A FEW D

CHAPTER ONE

THE CALL

Many adventures, such as this one, start with a single phone call.
That one call, just a few words, can often change the lives of many,
many people, some for the better, some for the worse.

It was a cold, cloudy day in early October with a few flakes of
snow blowing around when the old soldier received this particular
call.

Daniel Barker sat on a mountain a couple of miles from his home
fifteen miles from Cripple Creek Colorado. He had been following a
small herd of elk since shortly after sunrise but he wasn't really
hunting. He was just enjoying the scenery and life in general.

On the high point of a ridge that overlooked a narrow valley with a
little creek running through it, Barker stopped to take a break. It was
as pretty as any picture ever painted with the mountains topped off

by the gray clouds and the valley walls casting shadows in just the right places.

The wind was cold and he pulled his old gray Stetson down low and turned the collar of his sheep skin coat up against the cold wind. He had almost forgotten about the elk when his cell phone rang and he heard them take off from a rocky area just below him.

"Damn!" he muttered out loud as he pulled the noise maker out of his coat pocket. He looked at the number as it rang again and again. The incoming call was from a 662 area code which he knew was Mississippi, where he was originally from.

I wonder what's wrong he thought as he flipped it open.

"Hello?" he answered.

"Daniel?" The feminine voice sounded like it had some years on it.

"Yes ma'am, this is Daniel."

"This is your Aunt Annie Mae. How've ya'll been doing out there?" He hadn't heard a true southern accent in a long time and it brought a smile to his bearded face.

"Hey, Aunt Annie!" he answered cheerfully even though he was sure some bad news was close at hand. "I'm fine, just fine. How's everybody back home?"

"Oh, we're alright for the most part, but I've got some real bad news about your cousin, Tommy Ray." He and Tommy Ray Barker had been close growing up. They had hunted and fished, dated sisters and cousins and learned to drink beer and smoke cigarettes together. Aunt Annie paused and then went on. "Tommy Ray drove off the Highway 12 bridge on the Schooner River when he was on his way home from work yesterday." She paused for a moment, took a deep breath, and went on. "They pulled the truck out but they ain't found Tommy Ray yet."

This knocked the wind out of Barker.

"Aunt...Aunt Annie, I...I... uh, is there anything I can do?"

He could almost hear her shaking her head. "No, no. There's nothing right now. We're just waiting. But I did want to ask something of you."

"Anything, anything at all." He responded sincerely,

She cleared her throat. "I hate to be making plans like this but I was wondering if you could come back for the funeral if we get to have one. I know Tommy would've liked that and I want you to be a pall bearer, if you will."

Barker didn't have to think about it. "I'll be there."

"Good. We'll be looking for you as soon as you can get here." She answered in a sad, tired voice. "You be careful, now."

They chatted a little while before Barker closed up the phone, put it back in his pocket and started out along the valley rim at a long, steady walk. His mind was running wide open with questions that he wanted to ask his Aunt but he just didn't think this was the time. He wondered about the funeral if Tommy Ray wasn't there. In October the river would be getting cold and this could make it hard to find a body. The water level was also probably up and running fast from the fall rains and the Schooner could sweep a body thirty miles downstream before dropping it in Grenada Lake, the huge Corps of Engineers watershed reservoir the river emptied into.

He was also curious about the details of his cousin's death but there would be time for that later.

He stopped and watched five elk cross the creek at a gravel bar, then slung his rifle on his shoulder and headed toward home. He had his plans laid out when he got there.

The Farm, as he referred to his home, was an old eight hundred and fifty acre cattle ranch that had gone out of business twenty years before he found it. The ranch was in sad shape and he bought it from

4

the bank as a foreclosed property before refurbishing the old house and settling into a life of retirement. His favorite place in the house during the winter was in front of the huge fireplace that could burn firewood five feet long. He set it up with pot hangers on each side, a grill for the hearth and a couple of Dutch ovens. He cooked many a fine meal there and used it more than the gas stove in the kitchen when the weather was cool.

When he got to the house he threw enough clothes for the trip into a couple of bags, grabbed his good boots, a suit for the funeral, and headed back to the truck after locking up. He kept the sheep skin coat and well weathered cowboy hat on that he had worn up the mountain that morning. It would take a couple of days to drive to Mississippi and get there rested and ready for whatever the future brought and he wanted to get on the road as soon as possible. The snow was supposed to move out by nightfall and the trip should be a good one.

The next morning the weather had cleared and the bright, blue sky was a welcome sight.

Later that day, as Barker was pulling onto the highway after stopping for lunch his phone rang.

"Hello?" He answered.

"Danny?" Aunt Annie asked.

"Yes Ma'am?"

"I wanted to let you know that they, uh, found Tommy Ray a little while ago..." Her voice trailed off.

"I'm...I'm *so* sorry, Aunt Annie!" Barker said. His heart was breaking for her. Until now it seemed that Tommy Ray might come home at any time.

"It's going to be a closed casket funeral." She told him in a sad voice. "The Sheriff said that he had been in the water too long to have a viewing."

This bit of information bothered him a little but Barker didn't say anything. He'd find out more when he got there.

"I'm on my way, Aunt Annie. I'll be there as soon as I can, hopefully around supper time tomorrow." Dinner was still the noon meal for most people back home.

He heard her take a deep breath and let it out slow. "Be careful, Danny. I'll be lookin' for you."

Barker enjoyed driving. A good friend once told him that he must really like himself to be able to spend so much time alone.

And he had spent a lot of time alone in a lot of places around the world over the years, usually during a covert project.

He did a lot of thinking on this trip, mostly about growing up in Hendersonville Mississippi and Tommy Ray.

Hendersonville was in the northern hills of Mississippi, about a hundred miles southeast of Memphis and forty miles east of the flat, Mississippi delta. Most people there made their living logging, working in the lumber mills, or farming.

It was what people refer to as a sleepy little town with a town square that had huge shade trees on it, a court house in the center, and shops and stores around it. It *was* little, but it wasn't always sleepy.

It had come to life in the late 1800s when the Henderson Lumber and Land Company had built a railroad spur from the Illinois Central line in Coffeeville and ran it up the flat Schooner River bottom into thousands of acres of huge, virgin pine and hardwood timber. They set up a saw mill far enough from the river bank to avoid the spring floods and started turning the big trees into lumber. The first was used to build the mill offices, sheds and employees housing.

This also cleared the fertile bottom land that drew in the farmers and they were followed by the merchants who put in stores to sell the goods and services that were needed.

As soon as possible The Henderson Company built a two story company store. The square and streets were laid out using it as a corner anchor.

The store had three sections, hardware, dry goods and groceries downstairs with company offices upstairs. The employees, or hands as they were called, would buy what they needed there and charge it to an account which was paid for with money deducted from their weekly wages. If they weren't careful, the hands owed more money at the end of the week than they made.

Since everybody worked like dogs for five or six days a week, most people came to town on Saturday do their business and stock up on the supplies they needed. The town would be full of people and a lot of them would be ready to have some fun.

This 'fun' often came in the form of street dances or other tame entertainment but on occasion it turned wild.

There was very little law and very few lawmen around during those early days and drinking, gambling and fighting weren't hard to find.

As time marched on, Hendersonville grew and other industries moved in, along with a county school, churches and all the trappings of a real town. It was incorporated as such in 1923 and kept alive by the loggers, farmers and other enterprises, some of which weren't legal.

White Oak County, where Hendersonville was located, was a dry county and the boys started buying beer at one of the out of the way stores in the next county when they were fifteen years old and could drive across the county line. Before that somebody bought it for them or they bought it from one of the local bootleggers. There was one on each side of town. "Mr Billy" sold cheap whiskey in pint bottles and "Fats" sold beer in seven ounce 'pony' bottles.

They both started smoking a couple of years before that and somewhere along the way they learned to chew tobacco.

These days Barker was retired from his career as a Civilian Government Employee, or CGE and he spent his time now working on the Horse Ranch and driving around the country.

A lot of people are listed as CGEs and this covers everything from floor sweepers to rocket scientists. His specialties placed him somewhere in between these extremes with his duties falling around

9

the covert military and police work, sometimes far from U.S. borders and friendly forces. He had access to a lot of neat gear and information but he wasn't tied down with all of the legalities and rules that cops and soldiers were since a lot of the jobs he worked on never officially existed.

Barker sort of fell into this position shortly after joining the Army when he was eighteen, straight out of high school. After finishing boot camp and jump school at Fort Benning, Georgia, and excelling with both rifle and handgun, the young soldier was assigned to the range as an instructor. Even though he enjoyed being in near constant contact with weapons, he soon began to hate the monotony of the slow, methodic pace of teaching brainless recruits to use a very simple machine without killing themselves or somebody else during the process.

Barker would check out a beat up M14 rifle during his down time and spend all the time he could on the range all alone. On one of these days, while lying on his mat in the prone position, he saw a blue jay fly in and land on the top of a man size silhouette target at three hundred yards. The sky was clear, the sun bright, the wind calm and the shooter bored, all combined to cause Barker to calmly line the rifle up and squeeze the trigger.

His follow through was flawless and as the recoil subsided, he saw a handful of feathers in the air around the target's head. *Bingo!* He silent said to himself.

Barker cleared his weapon and gathered his gear. As he rose and turned he came face to face with a very stern faced officer.

"Shit!" the young soldier muttered to himself as he snapped to attention and started to salute.

"As you were!" the officer barked. "I'm Colonel Harold Ranson. We need to talk."

"Yes Sir!" Barker replied as he almost ran to catch up with the already walking officer.

"We have federal laws against shooting any kind of wildlife on military bases, Barker." Colonel Ranson said calmly. "But you knew that."

"Yes sir. I did." Barker answered.

"But you chose to kill that poor, dumb animal anyway. "Why?" Ranson asked as he stopped under a tree that offered plenty of shade.

Barker didn't have a *good* answer so he offered the first thing that came to him.

"It's, uh, because of my mother, sir."

Ranson didn't expect this. "Your mother?"

"Yes sir." Barker answered.

The colonel gave him a long hard look then ordered. "Explain."

The young soldier cocked his head to the right. "Well…" he drawled. "When I was a kid we had a big, old pecan tree in our yard. The blue jays would fly in there and eat all the pecans they could. Momma, er, my mother, would buy me all the BBs I needed to terrorize those birds. Then, later on, she kept me in four ten shotgun shells. She really hated those pecan thieves. I guess I feel the same way, sir."

"I read your file. Your Momma sounds like a fine woman." Ransom said. "I don't think you need to worry about that blue jay." He nodded toward the range. Then he handed Barker an envelope. "I want you to look this over and see what you think about it. It might be something you'd be interested in." He then turned and quickly walked away without another word.

After watching the colonel for a few seconds, Barker leaned against the oak and opened the envelope.

It outlined a program that was going to be offered to less than a hundred soldiers a chance to take a rigorous training course and then being assigned to a possibly hazardous project outside the United States. There wasn't much more information but it got Barker's attention and the next day he went to Colonel Ranson and asked to go to this program.

Two weeks later Barker packed his gear and headed for the tough training program in the hot, humid swamps and woods of Fort Polk Louisiana.

There he and the other volunteers were trained in the operation of a wide array of weapons from many countries but concentrating on the Soviet Bloc types. They were also subjected to some tough physical training and some off the wall tactics.

When this program ended, the students met with some "spooks", or secret agent types who asked for volunteers to go to a small country in a war torn section of southern Africa as advisors to help develop an army and to get the U.S. friendly leaders out before the bad guys got to them. Barker was the first to stand up and, at the ripe old age of eighteen and three forth years, was awarded the rank of commander.

He led a force of twenty four young, hard chargers through some awfully rough warfare for the next ten months.

Once on the ground it didn't take long to figure out that there were the good guys on one side, the bad guys on the other, and warlords leading little bands of cutthroats that were out to get whatever they could from both sides everywhere else. This caused a lot of confusion over who you were supposed to be shooting at. The lack of standard uniforms didn't help any, either.

Barker ordered his people to play by two main rules. 1. There were no rules. 2. If there was any doubt, refer back to rule 1. This worked out pretty well and kept most of them alive.

The bad guys were worse than anything Barker could dream up. Entire villages were raped, tortured, burned and hacked to death with machetes, except for the unfortunate few who were just hacked and allowed to live. There were amputees in nearly every village. Barker and his young, gung-ho Americans spent a year and a half there organizing an army and teaching them how to use weapons and tactics. The training was all on the job with little room for mistakes.

During this time they saw things on a daily basis that would cause Freddie Kruger and most of the other movie slasher boys to puke in their goalie masks.

After that mess in Africa simmered down, they were sent to help out in Central and South America. They referred to this area as somewhere south of Texas, since borders didn't mean much to them and a lot of the time they didn't know for sure what country they were in. But somebody was always happy to shoot at them and they were more than happy to shoot back, no matter where they were.

During the Africa and Central America forays, Barker had an old friend from back home, Michael Long, who was his right hand man. They nick named him Sarge even though he held no official rank. He and Barker entered into the belly of the beast more times that either man could count and they always managed to come back out, sometimes the worse for wear.

Sarge pulled out of the Army and went home to Hendersonville after they finished up down south. His father had cancer and his mother needed help back home.

While south of Texas, Barker worked with another young CGE by the name of Will Duncan. Will was a tall, lean farm boy from just outside of Springfield Missouri who was as tough as nails and could walk, run and fight just about anybody into the dirt. He returned to the States and wound up with an office in the Pentagon where he suffered spinal damage on September 11, 2001 at 0937 hours when American airlines Flight 77 crashed into the building near his office. But true to form, while hospitalized at Bethesda, Will had an office set up in his room and was back at work a few days after the attack. He kept Barker busy for quite a while with CGE jobs hunting down anybody who were involved in any kind of terrorism until the old warrior decided to retire.

Will was always real handy to have around because he had a lot of pull with military and law enforcement around the world and a huge toy box to draw from.

On this trip back home, like any other, Barker's truck carried not only himself and clothes but it also carried a midsized arsenal tucked here and there. He was a firm believer in the old adage that it's better to have it and not need it than to need it and not have it. Barker had most of it.

He grew up thinking that everybody's momma had a pistol in her purse because his always did and he started keeping a handgun close at hand when he was fifteen. It wasn't because he was a bad ass or that he ran with a bad crowd. They were just tools to be kept close and used when needed.

The trip was a good one and he made extra good time, arriving in Hendersonville just past one o'clock.

Home Again

Barker drove slowly down the quiet street and stopped in front of Aunt Annie Mae's house.

It was a large white frame house with a steep tin roof and a porch extending across the entire front and one end. There were ancient rose bushes and other colorful, fragrant plants around the yard along with huge pecan and oak shade trees and a long drive way curving lazily to the right side of the house.

Several cars and pickups lined the driveway and more were parked on the neatly mowed grass of the large front yard.

Barker surveyed the scene and said out loud to himself "I bet a lot of fine, young, chickens gave their lives for the cause." He was thinking of the old southern tradition of friends and family bringing food to the home of the deceased loved one. Fried chicken was usually the main dish because back in the day, everybody had yard chickens and knew how to fry up a couple on short notice. It also keeps well for a couple of days and can be eaten cold or easily warmed up. This made it easy for a grieving family member to have an easy meal any time day or night.

He drove over the short curb and parked on the far edge of the yard away from the other vehicles.

As he got out, he was met by a big, friendly black and tan hound dog.

"Hello Ranger." He said to the old dog. Barker hadn't met this particular dog before, but Tommy Ray had named every dog he ever owned Ranger so it wasn't hard to figure out. Then he heard a voice call from the shaded area near the back of the house.

"Ya'll come on back out here and sit for a while after you make your appearance inside. There ain't nobody in the house as interesting as me."

It was his uncle, Detrick Barker, but everybody called him Det. He was a World War Two veteran, a retired cop and somewhat of a local hero. He had a box full of medals and citations that he liked to talk about to anybody who would listen and he did it in more of an educational way than something that sounded like bragging.

Det also carried an ever present walking cane that he used because of injuries he got during the war as old age and arthritis caught up him. It was all beat up from years of whipping bad dogs, misbehaving kids and stupid grownups.

19

Barker was glad to see Det, partly because his uncle was getting old and probably wouldn't be around too many more years, but mainly because he was his favorite uncle. It was his war stories that made the younger Barker consider a military career all those years before.

Det was sitting in a porch swing that had been hung on the lowest limb of a huge pecan tree with heavy log chains so long ago that the links had grown deep into the wood. The swing itself had been painted every time anything else around the house got painted and had a thick, impervious coat of protection that would probably never let it rot. It was a regular family heirloom.

"It's good to see you, Uncle Det." Barker said as he shook his uncle's eighty year old hand that was still strong enough to hurt you. "How are you doing?"

Uncle Det hooked his walking cane over his right shoulder. "Well, I feel that German shrapnel in my right leg from 1943 every time a rain's coming, my back still bothers me from when we parachuted into France in 1944, my left hip and shoulder hurts from that damn drunk that t-boned me at the red light by the Piggly Wiggly store a few years back, and my dick ain't worked right for the last week or so. Other than that, I'm doing pretty good for an old man."

Barker laughed. "Glad to hear it!"

After stepping inside to let Aunt Annie know he had made it and see some familiar faces, Barker slipped out, took a straight chair from the porch and joined his uncle at the swing. Det asked him all about things out west and they caught up on some old times.

After a while they heard a bicycle bell ringing in a steady ring-ring, ring-ring as it came up the street getting nearer and nearer.

Det looked down the street before saying "Here comes your retarded buddy you was in the Army with." Then after a long pause he added in a low voice. "That boy ain't right, you know."

Barker turned slowly and saw a blue Pee Wee Herman type bicycle coming their way. It was hauling a slight built man wearing a red plaid flannel, long sleeve shirt with all of the buttons buttoned up tight, along with faded jeans and red Converse high tops. A green John Deere baseball cap was pulled down to his eyebrows.

Barker inhaled deep and let it out. "Yeah, I know, Uncle Det. But me and him saved each other's asses more times that I can count. He's one of the bravest men I ever knew."

The bike coasted into the yard and the rider dropped the kick stand. He approached Barker, extended his hand and said "It's good to see you, Cap'n."

Barker grasped his hand tightly and replied genuinely, "It's good to see you too, Sarge."

They sat in the yard until almost sundown and visited with several other people who came and went. They also did away with several cold Budweiser's and most of a bottle of Jack Daniels. This was the Mississippi form of the Irish wake.

When Barker started to leave, Sarge followed him to his truck and called him aside.

"I need to talk to you for a minute." He said quietly.

"Okay. How about here?" Barker asked.

Sarge quickly scanned the area and said "Cap'n, your cousin didn't drown in the Schooner."

Barker stood silent for a moment waiting on the punch line. Finally he asked simply "What?"

"I said…" Sarge started but Barker cut him off.

"I heard you the first time. " Barker's curiosity was up. "What do you mean, he didn't drown?"

"Well, I was in the funeral home yesterday getting a bottle of whiskey from Lenard, you know, the undertaker, and I saw Tommy Ray's body. There was a bullet hole in his head." Sarge said seriously.

Barker processed this information for a few seconds then asked "You get your whiskey at the funeral home?"

"Well, yeah. But is that all you heard?" Sarge seemed aggravated.

Barker held up a hand. "Sorry, you're right. Are you sure it's a bullet hole?"

Sarge turned his head a little to the right. "I think I've seen enough of them in enough folks over the years to recognize one when I see it. Don't you?"

He was right. The two of them had seen more than their fair share of high velocity puncture wounds on battle fields in their time. "Yeah, I do. Tell me about this one." Barker answered.

Sarge leaned against the bed of the truck. "Like I said, I went by there to get a bottle. Old Lenard keeps a case or two of pretty good whiskey around that he peddles out."

"You mean Old Lenard Morris is bootlegging?" Barker asked.

Lenard Morris had been the town undertaker for the last fifty years or so. The story was that Lenard had learned the trade while assigned to a graves registration unit when he was in the Army and stationed in Korea during that war. He started out as a medic but for some reason he didn't do too well in the medical field and he was transferred to work with dead soldiers instead of live ones. He was more than a little weird, like a lot of morticians were.

"Yeah. He has been for years." Sarge replied. "Anyway, I guess he didn't hear me when I walked in on him in the embalming room because when he saw me, he zipped up Tommy Ray's body bag real quick. When he went get my bottle I peeked in there."

Sarge was kind of unique, to say the least. He missed a lot of school and attended some of the remedial classes but Mike "Sarge" Moore was the best person you could ask for to have on your side when the shit got thick. And Barker had never known him to run his mouth about anything that he didn't know something about.

Barker let this sink in for a minute before asking. "What did you see?"

Sarge put his left index finger on his left temple. "There was a hole right there. It was small, probably a .22. I didn't have time to look for anything else. And another thing, he hadn't been in no water."

Barker shot him a hard look. "Are you sure?"

"He was dry as a bone, hair, clothes and all!"

Barker stood still and quiet, thinking about what he had just heard. After a long pause Sarge asked in a voice just above a whisper. "What are you going to do about this?"

That was a damn good question.

"I, uh, don't know." He looked at Sarge. "Do you have any ideas?"

Sarge smiled and answered enthusiastically in a hushed child like voice. "Yeah! We do a night-op and sneak into the funeral home and you can see for yourself."

"Whoa! Slow down a little!" Barker replied. "Give me a minute to think about this. Who would want to kill Tommy Ray?"

Sarge scratched his chin. "I'm not sure but that's something that needs figured out!"

"I tell you what, why don't you come by the motel later and you can catch me up on everything." He told Sarge. There was no need to tell him *which* motel since there was only one in town.

Sarge swung a leg over his bike. "Sounds good to me. See you later, Cap'n."

Barker thought back to the reason that Reid gave Aunt Annie for the closed casket. Now he finds out that Tommy Ray hadn't been in the water at all. Maybe Sarge or Aunt Annie or *somebody* had their facts wrong. But wet or dry, Barker believed that Sarge saw a bullet hole in Tommy Ray and that meant that whatever was going on, Lenard was in it. And maybe the good sheriff, too.

Barker drove through Hendersonville on his way to the motel. He wanted to see the old home town but he was also mulling over Sarge's story. He wanted to hear what else his old friend had to say tonight before he started breaking into any spooky old funeral home.

An hour after dark, Sarge showed up and filled him in on what had been happening around White Oak County for the last several years.

It seemed that an old schoolmate of Barker's by the name of Jack Reid was the sheriff these days. Reid had been the star quarterback for the last three years of high school and dated the head cheerleader, Tammy Wallace. Reid was a mediocre ball player and Tammy was a pretty good whore with a killer teenage body topped off by a pair of huge tits. Barker wondered what the years and gravity had done to her.

Reid's best buddy was Harry Pope, the school bully. When Reid was elected to office he brought Pope on as his chief deputy, the second in command.

The good sheriff won the job when the former one had left office early because of a bout with cancer. Then he had been re-elected by huge margins for the next five terms. Nearly every other elected county official had also stayed in office without any trouble. And they all seemed to be doing real well on their meager county salaries.

Barker and Sarge drove to the Highway 12 bridge where Tommy Ray supposedly drove into the river. Yellow crime scene tape was still tied across the area but they didn't let it keep them from looking everything over, even though there wasn't much to see. There had been a huge amount of foot traffic and it didn't look like any attempt was made to preserve the scene. It really wasn't necessary since Tommy Ray's death was deemed an accident right off the bat and not a murder.

On the way there, Barker listened to everything that Sarge had to say. Most of it didn't mean anything alone but when you start put it

27

all together, it did seem like something shady was going on. But it still didn't explain why or even if Tommy Ray had anything to do with it.

"What about our little night-op?" Sarge asked when he finished.

"I...don't know." Barker answered slowly. This needed to be thought through. He would hate to miss his cousin's funeral because he was sitting in jail on a breaking and entering charge.

"Look, Tommy Ray's getting buried the day after tomorrow." Sarge said. "We ain't got much time. Once they put him in that grave, it'll take an act of congress to get him and that bullet back out of the ground."

Barker thought about it a minute before giving in. Sarge was right. Hell, it might even be fun.

Midnight found Barker and Sarge sneaking through alleys and empty lots to get to Morris and Sons Funeral Emporium without anybody seeing them. They worked their way to the rear of the old two story house where Sarge opened a window and started to climb inside.

"You seem to know your way around here a little too good." Barker whispered.

Sarge ignored him and went on in. A few seconds later he opened a nearby door and let Barker in.

The door led into the work area on the back of the building. Inside the air had a strong, chemical smell of formaldehyde that seemed to stick to you. There was also a smell of death that the old house would probably hold onto forever.

The funeral parlor had a big round clock with a blue neon light around the face mounted on the roof of the front porch that cast an eerie glow on everything around and it gave the interior of the building a real unique look, casting eerie black and gray shadows throughout the building.

As they made their way down a hall, Barker noticed that Sarge was strolling along without a care in the world.

"Aren't you worried about them hearing you?" Barker whispered.

"Who?" Sarge asked in a normal voice.

Barker pointed up.

"God?" Sarge asked.

"No! Lenard!" Barker hissed, trying to keeping his voice low.

Sarge waved a hand. "Naw. They built a big, fine house out by Grenada Lake a few years ago. Ain't nobody here but us and Tommy Ray, unless Lenard hauled somebody else in."

A little further down the hall Sarge couldn't help but grab Barker by the arm who instinctively started to go into a defensive crouch and asked in a hushed whisper, "What is it?"

Sarge said seriously, cutting his eyes from side to side. "Listen! I think I hear one of them silent alarms!"

Barker gave his old NCO a long, hard look as he slowly rose back to his full height and walked away shaking his head.

"Hee! Hee!" Sarge giggled. "That never gets old!"

They stopped at a large, walk in refrigerator and opened the door. The cold room was empty except for a single, ornate, wooden casket on a four wheel carriage. Barker tried to raise the lid but it wouldn't budge.

"Here, you'll need this." Sarge was holding a key, a small wrench used to lock the lid down. Barker took it and in a minute the lid was raised and they were looking at a black body bag.

As his old captain unzipped it, Sarge sighed and, while waving a hand to dissipate the odor, said "Man! I hope your Aunt Annie Mae didn't pay for embalming 'cause he ain't been embalmed."

Barker finished opening the bag and was met by his dead cousin's blank stare. He shined the small flashlight on the gray, waxy face for a moment then, holding his cousin's chin, turned Tommy Ray's head and looked at the left temple. There, just as Sarge had said, was a small, round, blue wound with a black hole in the middle of it. The skin around it was damaged and covered with black specks.

"He was shot up close." Barker mumbled.

He turned Tommy Ray's head and looked for any other wounds and while he found no holes, he did find a soft place low over his right ear. "One way in. No way out." He said to himself.

Barker then took a piece of wire about a foot long that he had clipped from a coat hanger in his motel room and inserted it slowly into the bullet hole. He was able to slide it easily through the wound channel to the skull on the other side where the soft spot was without any trouble.

Sarge watched his old friend at work. "Well? What do you think?"

"He was shot, alright." Barker said. "Looks like the bullet hit the skull on the other side hard enough to crack it but not hard enough to penetrate it. It probably bounced around in there before it ran out of steam."

"So the bullet's still in there?" Sarge asked.

"Looks that way." Barker replied.

Sarge looked at Tommy Ray, then back at Barker. "Are we going to take it out?"

Barker shook his head as he snapped a few quick pictures with his cell phone and checked Tommy Ray's clothes, which were, indeed, dry. Then he re-zipped the bag. "It's good where it is. If we can get enough evidence to start something, we'll have Tommy Ray dug up. The bullet will be safe and sound right where it is till then."

The two left the building the way they came in and were soon strolling down a sidewalk near the town square. The October night was cool, the bugs were quiet and there were no buzzing mosquitoes. Barker enjoyed the walk and his memories of the little town but right now his mind was busy with what he just saw.

On the way back to the motel, Sarge told Barker all about Reid and his crooked ways.

"How does he stay in office?" Barker asked.

"Well, it's kind of a funny thing," Sarge answered as he turned his head a little sideways. "Do you remember his Aunt Fay?"

"Yeah." Barker replied. "He lived with her when we were growing up, didn't he?"

Sarge nodded. "That's right. His momma was her sister. After his momma died in a car wreck when he was just a little kid Fay took him in and raised him as her own. Well, old Faye's the circuit clerk these days and runs the county election commission. Hell, she knows more about those voting machines than the service techs from the factory."

Barker laughed a little. "You're kidding?"

Sarge shook his head. "Nope. She goes to California where the machines are made and takes a so called maintenance class at least once a year. Probably parties her ass off while she's out there. The damn things only get used every four years. She keeps them tuned up so they all stay in office."

"You mean, Fay and Reid, Right?" Barker asked.

Sarge smiled. "Nope. I mean every elected official in the county."

"You can't mean all of them! They're all in on it?" Barker asked.

Sarge started counting on his fingers. "I mean the sheriff, the county clerk, the tax collector, all of the supervisors, everybody." He paused a minute. "His cousin, Jimmy, is the chief of police here in Hendersonville and he's got his head so far up Reid's ass that the only thing sticking out is a pair of cowboy boots, so Reid's pretty much running the town cops, too."

"Is Jimmy in on everything with Reid?" Barker asked.

"I don't think so." Sarge answered. "Jimmy's too damn lazy to do much of anything he ain't got to. He just walks around town all day in his pretty, pressed uniform and visits with all the business folks. Everybody says he's working his way up to be mayor. Then they'll have the town *and* the county all sewed up."

There was no doubt that this thing was bigger than they could handle. Maybe Will Duncan would be willing to help out.

The two decided that they would go to the funeral home tomorrow night for visitation, and the funeral the next day. Then Barker would hang around and see what he could find out. He could use the cover of being a land broker that scouted out old farms and other land for investors all over the country. This would give him freedom to look

34

around and talk to a lot of people without raising much suspicion. It had worked before in other places. It would work here, too.

 Barker would call Will in the morning and let him know about this and see if there was anything he could do. He was ram rodding the CGEs and he had access to all of the data bases that any government agency had and a lot of manpower at his disposal. He was as handy as a pocket on a shirt to have around.

"I've got an idea as to how we can get this thing started, but it'll shock the hell out of some folks and might cause a heart attack or two." Sarge said a little excited.

"How's that?" Barker asked.

"When ya'll start out of the funeral home with the casket, drop it on that concrete drive way at the back of the hearse. Tommy Ray rolls out and everybody gets a good look at him and his bullet hole and this whole thing is blowed wide open!"

 Barker stared at Sarge for a minute and then replied. "And then we just scoop up poor old Aunt Annie because she'll be the first one that has a heart attack and we bury her in Tommy Ray's place." He shook his head. "I don't think so. We'll just look and listen for a while."

Sarge looked at the ground and muttered. "Well, I never said it was a perfect plan."

THE CEMETARY

AT

OLD ANTIOCH

Barker was having a little trouble believing this county had gotten as corrupt as his old friend believed it was. This was the kind of thing that happened in movies or foreign countries. Not in the good ole U S of A!

Then, almost without thinking, he heard himself ask "Is there anything else?"

"Well…" Sarge drawled. "There *is* the cemetery up at Old Antioch."

Old Antioch was a little wood frame church at the end of a dead end, gravel road on a high ridge north of town. Starting a few feet from the west wall of the church was a cemetery full of ancient cedar trees and graves dating back to the early 1800s. It was a long drive out there over rough, winding roads during good weather and slick, muddy ones in bad.

It was one of the oldest churches in the county that came to be when there was still a fairly dense population in the heavily wooded hill area. But the people of the area began to move into the river bottom to farm the fertile land there that was made more accessible as the old virgin timber was cleared to feed the Henderson mill in the early twentieth century. By the 1950s the hills and hollers were pretty much void of any full time human inhabitants. The little church was used less and less until 1967 when the small congregation decided to cease regular church services and only have a homecoming there on the first Sunday after Easter each year.

"What about Old Antioch?' Barker asked patiently.

"Oh, about seven or eight years ago I was huntin' up there on an old horse I had."Sarge started. "I tied him to a bush and slipped down a white oak holler nice and quiet-like, thought I might kill me a couple of fox squirrels…"

"Is this going to be a long story?" Barker asked as he massaged his forehead.

Sarge grinned. "Long enough! But it'll be worth it."

He continued. "So I'm being real quiet and waaaay off in the distance I heard a truck coming up out of the bottom so I stopped and listened."

"It's pulling pretty hard so I knew it had a load on it. I decided to run up to the top of the ridge because I could see the road through the trees since the leaves had all fell and in a minute or two I seen it." Sarge paused.

Barker waited a moment, then leaned forward and asked. "Seen what?"

"A flat bed one ton truck pulling one of them little track hoes on a trailer." He answered.

Barker waited for Sarge to continue but he just sat there with his arms crossed.

"So…maybe he was going up there to dig a hole." Barker offered. "People do that with track hoes."

Sarge shook his head violently. "Nope! Uh-uh! Not up there!"

"Why not?" Barker asked. "There *is* a cemetery up there and graves are just high priced holes, you know?"

"But Lenard was following it in his hearse!" Sarge answered excitedly. "Get it?"

Barker shook his head. "Look, old buddy. I need you to slow down and fill in *all* the empty spaces for me. OK?"

Sarge rolled his eyes and raised his arms above his head. "It's as simple as it can be!"

"Look! Just finish the story!" Barker gave Sarge a hard look. It had been a long day, what with driving into town, breaking into a funeral home and looking at your dead cousin with a bullet hole in his head. Barker was a *little* tired.

Sarge sat up very straight, took in a deep breath and exhaled slowly. "Ok." He said calmly. "I sat up there for about an hour and a half and they came back down the road, headed toward town." He looked at Barker and smiled a little kid smile. "So I went and got Old Thunder. That was my horse's name, by the way."

Barker nodded slowly.

"Well, after they got out of hearing distance, me and Old Thunder rode up to the graveyard and there was a brand new grave. They even stuck one of them little temporary brass signs in the ground at the head of it with the dearly departed's name on it You know, they cast them in a foundry and the letters are part of the sign itself."

"And what did the little brass sign say?" Barker's patience was running short.

Sarge leaned forward and squinted his eyes as if he was reading that very sign right now. "It said *Paul Michal Goddard, Born February 18, 1960, Died August 1, 1976."*

Barker was tired and he needed some sleep, and the only part of his body that would move right now were the little wheels in his brain, some of which were rusty and choked with cob webs. But they all began to turn. Slowly at first, then faster. And faster still until they slung the dirt and crud off and began to run smoothly.

Barker cocked his head to the right and looked at Sarge. "Are you sure?"

The old soldier nodded confidently. "Then I went to Hendersonville Memorial Gardens and checked." Sarge leaned forward and rested his elbows on his knees. "And there was his tombstone, right where he was buried when we were in high school and he missed Dead Man's Curve and smacked that big oak tree." Paul Goddard was a school mate of Barker and Sarge who was killed in a car crash on that warm, humid, summer night while they were out of school for summer break.

41

Barker's gaze did not move from Sarge. After a long silence, Sarge said "I told you it would be worth it."

Barker laced his fingers together, placed his hands behind his head and leaned back in the chair.

"Surely they didn't move Paul up there!?" It came out as much as a question as a statement.

"Naw." Sarge answered. "Like I said, that was seven or eight years ago. Before that there hadn't been a new grave in there since Ms Allie Kincaid was buried back in '87. But I drove back up there once in a while after that and there was a new grave every six months or so and they all had those little signs stuck in the ground. And guess what! They all had somebody's name on it that was buried somewhere else.. I know. I checked them out."

Barker perked up. "What did you do? Dig them up?'

Sarge laughed and waved his hand. "Naw! But I did go by the hardware store and get a ten foot long stick of quarter inch cold rolled steel rod and sharpened the end. Then I took it up there and drove it into that fresh grave until it hit something solid, like a coffin lid. And do you know what I found?" He asked with a twinkle in his eye.

42

Barker slowly shook his head.

"About a foot of rod stickin' up out of the ground." He answered flatly.

"So…" Barker drawled. "If there was a casket in there and the top was nine feet deep, then the grave was actually dug around eleven feet deep."

"That's right." Sarge answered as he waited patiently.

"That's a lot of hole to dig." Barker thought for a second. "Why would you bury somebody that deep?"

"I think I've got that part figured out." Sarge answered happily. "Let's say you wanted get rid of a body, a murder victim or somebody you just didn't want to show up ever again. No body usually means no conviction."

"You could throw it in a river or try to burn it up but something might go wrong and somebody might find it. That shit happens all the time on TV." Sarge explained."And you would need to do it quiet-like, so it wouldn't get no attention drawn to it. What would be better than in the bottom of a very deep grave?"

Barker was confused. "I don't follow you."

"Then…" Sarge continued, ignoring Barker. "You could bury somebody else on top of them later, a *legitimate* burial and the first body would probably be there forever and nobody would ever find it. You've got three feet of dirt between the two caskets so the grave digger wouldn't have no reason to dig into the first one. Now, you used your own grave digger for the deep hole, you would probably use the same one for the second one, too, so nobody else would know. Then, if a rumor *did* get out about somebody being buried under Grandma Johnson, nobody would believe it and it'd be harder than hell to get her dug up just to see if she was bunkin' in there with somebody else."

Barker let this sink in a minute and said. "That's a pretty good story there…"

"Wait a minute!" Sarge continued. "I ain't through just yet. These graves kept showing up and Lenard had a few *real* funerals up there from time to time so I went to see an old friend of mine in the archeology department over at Auburn University and talked him into loaning me one of those ground penetrating radar sets."

"Find anything?" Barker asked.

Sarge nodded. "Since I found that first grave, there's been a total of fourteen bodies buried and only three or four are the real deal. One was an old woman that grew up around there and had family buried in the cemetery. The others are folks Lenard talked into Old Antioch by giving them a good deal on the funeral."

"Who was the guy in the truck when you saw them?" Barker asked. "He's in on this, Too."

"Gal."

"Gal?"

"Gal." Sarge repeated.

"Ok. Who's the gal?" Barker asked.

"April."

"April? Lenard's daughter?"

"Yeah." Sarge said with a look on his face like he tasted something bad. "She's got a construction company between here and Tupelo. That girl always gave me the creeps." He suddenly shook as if a chill had just crossed his body.

"One more thing." Barker stated. "Why use Paul's sign?"

"Probably too cheap to get one made." Sarge answered. "When they bury somebody they stick that temporary sign in the ground. Then, when the tombstone gets delivered, they pull that temporary sign up and pitch it in a fifty five gallon drum in a shed behind the funeral home. They probably just reached in and grabbed one. I bet they never thought anybody would take notice."

Barker rubbed his eyes, suddenly very tired. "Well, if everybody else in this county gets away with whatever they're doing, I believe a *blind* cop could get a conviction on Lenard Morris."

Sarge and Barker talked a while longer before calling it a night. The eastern sky was starting to show a little light as the two old soldiers finished up.

"I'll call Will and run this past him after I get a few hours sleep." Barker told Sarge. "Maybe we can get the ball rolling pretty quick."

"That would be great." Sarge answered as he mounted his bike. "I'll be around the house if you need me."

Then as he started to pedal away, Barker yelled at him. "Hey! How come you haven't done anything about this before now?"

Sarge stopped and looked back at his old friend. "I don't know. Probably because you're the only person I ever really trusted." Then he shrugged his shoulders and pedaled off into the gray dawn.

Barker smiled at this answer. He and Sarge both had each other's backs in some mighty tight places over the years and neither one had ever doubted the other.

Barker slowly turned and went into his room where he was soon sound asleep. It was good to be home for a while.

Day 2

A couple of hours later Barker awoke to the sounds of traffic on Highway 12 outside his motel room. This was the busy two lane main highway of the area and the loggers, farmers and other working people were out in force this morning.

He got a shower and was soon pulling onto the road with everybody else. A few minutes later Barker stopped by the Kettle Family Restaurant for breakfast. While he was waiting on his order, Sheriff Jack Reid and his wife came in.

Well, lookie here! Barker said to himself. *Time to go to work.*

Barker waved at them and Reid looked at him a few seconds before recognizing him. Then he greeted him like a long, lost friend.

"Hey, Hon!" Tammy squealed as she gave Barker a big hug that was just a little too touchy-feely. He could hardly breathe through the loud perfume she had doused herself in as she held him extra tight and pressed her big store bought titties against him.

After Barker finally separated himself from her, Reid shook his hand and they exchanged their pleasantries.

The three sat in a booth and the Reids ordered breakfast. Then, while they waited on their meal, they told him how sorry they were about Tommy Ray and offered to help Aunt Annie Mae in any way that they could. Then Tammy asked in her bubbly, ex-cheerleader voice. "So, what are you doing for yourself these days?"

"I'm in the land brokerage business." Barker answered.

"How does that work?" Reid asked as he poured cream and sugar into his coffee.

Barker tried to sound important. "I travel around the country and look for old farms and acreage or old factories or any other kind of real estate for sale and match it up with people that want it for investments or hunting clubs and such."

Reid seemed to be really interested. "Is there good money in something like that?"

"Oh, yeah! Especially now! Big money folks are standing in line with cash in hand waiting on me to find something for them to buy." Barker said it like he meant it.

This *really* got Reid's attention since he had 'acquired' several pieces of property by less than legal means during his time in office. He didn't really start out to do this, but it was just *so damn easy*, what with him being the top law enforcement officer in the county. A lot of people trusted him with everything they owned, no questions asked. Reid started out just taking a little but as time went on he took a little more…then a little more…and before long, money and property were stacked up everywhere with the sheriff's name on it. This might be a good time to turn some of the land into cold, hard cash. He could use Barker to do all the paper work and keep his name out of it. And besides, if things did go south, what better fall guy than a returning home boy who was stressed out from losing his favorite cousin?

"Well, uh, maybe you ought to hang around after the funeral and look at some property around here. I could point you toward some that old folks own and they ain't got anybody to take over after they're gone. You might even be able to pick some up from the county for the delinquent taxes." Reid said. "I might even have a couple of pieces of land that I'd part with…if the price was right."

Barker thought for a second. "Wouldn't I have to bid on something like that when it came up for sale?" He asked.

Reid smiled. "Aw, there's always a loop hole for everything, if you know what I mean."

I've got a pretty good idea. Barker thought to himself.

"I could probably get you a finder's fee if you could help me out with some of this." Barker said as he worked the bait.

"Well…" Ried started slowly. "That might not be exactly legal *or* ethical, me being the sheriff and all…"

Maybe I was wrong about him… Barker thought.

"…but if you could make it all cash…"

He smiled. *Nope. He's crooked.*

"…then I'm sure I could help you out." The sheriff smiled broadly.

"I don't think cash would be a problem." Barker said as he set the hook deep.

"I tell you what," Reid said. "I know it may not be exactly right with you just losing your cousin and all, but I believe in striking while the iron is hot. How about you and me ride out Highway 12 and look at a couple of pieces of land tomorrow afternoon after the funeral? Might be something some of your clients would be interested in."

"That's a good idea." Barker Answered. "I'll check with Aunt Annie and see if she needs anything and I'll let you know for sure. It'll be good to see some of the old stomping grounds again."

After eating a hearty breakfast, the three walked to the parking lot and Reid and Tammy left.

Reid was in deep thought as he drove toward his office in the courthouse on the town square. You could almost hear the wheels turning in his head.

"A penny for your thoughts, Hon." Tammy said as she put her sunglasses on.

Reid smiled as he pushed against the steering wheel to stretch a few muscles.

"Just thinking about old Daniel Barker, there." He said.

Me, too! Thought Tammy.

Barker was never in their little clique in school, what with she being the head cheerleader and going steady with the quarterback. Barker never played sports but he had an air about him that always got her attention. He was so damn independent!

She would talk Jack Reid into taking her to any local rodeo that popped up because she knew Barker would be there taking some of the top money in the saddle bronc competitions. Jack would bitch about having to go but Tammy would talk about how she just loved the horses, and he would finally give in and take her.

And any time she heard a motorcycle coming down the road, she had to check to see if it was Barker. He rode motorcycles from the time they were in junior high school until he left for the army. He didn't ride with any kind of gang and the loner thing gave him a bad boy image that drew her to him back then... *and* now.

She watched and waited for several of her teenage years but was never able to get close enough to him to make anything happen between them.

The best chance she ever got was on a cold Saturday at the annual Christmas parade of their senior year as the floats and the bands were lining up at the high school. The last entrants were the horses and she knew Barker would be there. He always rode in the parade. Tammy was going to be riding a float with the rest of the cheerleaders and the football team. She told Reid she was going to see the horses and even asked him to go with her.

"I'm not going to see those stinking ass horses!" was his answer. "I'm staying here with the team!"

"Fine!" She told him. "I'll go by myself!"

A few minutes later she found Barker beside his trailer throwing a saddle on a big sorrel. She quickly glanced around to make sure nobody was watching and nervously approached the young cowboy.

"H...hi Danny!" she stammered.

Barker froze for a second then slowly turned to her, a little smile on his face. His gaze slowly traveled from her face to her sweater, where her nipples were straining against the fabric, then on to her toes and back to her face.

"Tammy." He said as he nodded politely. "Did you, uh...*lose* Reid?" he asked. His voice was deep for a teenager and it touched her down deep.

"No! He...he's at the float!" she answered, her voice weak.

Barker turned to the horse and started to cinch up the saddle.

With his back to her, he spoke seriously. "If he catches you over here, I'll have to kill him *and* Pope because I ain't taking no ass whooping for you."

After screwing the saddle down tight, Barker turned back toward Tammy.

Without warning she rushed to him, threw her arms around his neck and planted a kiss on his mouth. Not just a little peck but a hard deep wet kiss with lots of tongue.

His honed reflexes kicked in and he wrapped his arms around her and held her tight, giving back what she was giving. Tammy hesitated a half second then ground herself into him.

The smell of the horse, the leather and the cowboy was adding to the moment. Then, through the perfect moment, she heard it.

"Tammy! Where are you?" It was Charlotte Jones, one of the cheerleaders.

Barker slowly broke the kiss and smiled as he turned toward his horse. "Sounds like you're being paged."

"Damn!" Tammy glanced in the direction of the voice. "I've got to go!"

"Me too." Barker answered as he stuck his boot into the stirrup and swung a leg over the saddle.

Tammy stepped forward and started to say something.

"Tammy! There you are!" Charlotte called from a few feet away. "Come on! We need to practice our cheers before the parade starts!"

Barker had a sly grin on his face as he looked back at Tammy, touched the brim of his Stetson and rode away to join the other riders. Tammy tried to watch him but Charlotte was making that nearly impossible.

And Barker was right. Reid and Pope would beat the hell out of him if they found out about what just happened. And he would have killed them both.

The parade seemed to last forever but as soon as the float was parked back at the school Tammy slipped away and went to find Barker. But when she arrived at the gravel lot, his truck and trailer were gone. He had already loaded up and left.

Over the next few months Tammy watched for another opportunity to see Barker but it never happened. She and Reid were busy doing the popular senior student things right up until graduation and Barker was doing whatever it was that he did.

Then Barker headed off to the army, only to return home for short visits. By that time, Tammy and Jack were married and the Barker door seemed closed forever.

Shortly after getting hitched the Reids moved to Memphis for a year where Jack buddied up with an unsavory character named Ray Gantz. He owned several night clubs around The Big M and was rumored to be involved with prostitution, drugs and all kinds of other bad hobbies. It looked as if he was going to take Jack on as a partner and the newlyweds would be living in a big house in the big city with all the fineries that big money could buy. But best of all, they wouldn't be in poe-dunk Mississippi any more.

That suited Tammy just fine. She didn't care where the fame and fortune came from as long as it came.

Then Gantz and Jack came up with this idea about the Reids moving back and Jack running for sheriff the next year. She never understood how this was supposed to be a good thing but she wasn't given a voice in the plan. The boys made all the decisions and they let her know this up front.

Soon Tammy found herself back in the sticks and having to help her husband get elected by smiling and pretending to be glad to see all of those people she was so happy to have gotten away from.

Then when Reid won the election, she felt like she had been sentenced to life in the boondocks and a huge door had slammed behind her.

But when Ray and his money showed up from time to time, it became easier to play her part. And with the respect and power that her husband's position as top lawman in the county brought, Tammy could look down on the people she despised.

She still thought of Daniel Barker from time to time. When she read an article in the local paper that he had retired from the military or whatever it was he did, and was living in Colorado, she thought about trying to contact him. She went as far as writing a letter and held onto it for several months. But before she could find Barker's address and mail it to him, she met Silvie Tower.

Silvie was a beautiful black girl with fine features and a body that was the envy of men *and* women. She was also a lot younger than Tammy. They met in the parking lot of the Piggly Wiggly grocery store on a cold, rainy, winter's day.

Silvie was parked beside Tammy and her car wouldn't start. Tammy felt sorry for her and, since they only lived a short distance apart, offered Silvie a ride home.

As Tammy drove along the highway, she couldn't help but steal a glance at Silvie's big, erect nipples straining against the wet cloth of her blouse.

"If you like what you see, just keep lookin'." Silvie suddenly said.

Tammy was surprised and embarrassed. "I…I don't know what you're talking about!" She stammered as she struggled to stare straight ahead.

"You don't have to worry, honey!" Silvie cooed as she unbuttoned her blouse. "I ain't gonna' tell *anybody* and I'm sure you won't either." She unhooked her bra between the cups and leaned back, letting her big tits speak for themselves.

Tammy timidly turned and looked at Silvie. She had never really been with another woman before, although she had 'experimented' with a few friends as a teenager. But right now she couldn't think of anything she wanted more that to have her way with the woman sitting beside her.

"I've been watching you for a long time, Ms Reid." Silvie said in a sultry voice. "I hear all the stories about your husband and his girlfriends. I could be *your* girlfriend. And you could do anything you want to with me. I could fill in all those empty places in your life and make you happy." Silvie's hand took Tammy's and squeezed it gently. *"Real* happy."

Tammy drove them to Silvie's empty house where the two women explored and made love to each other for several hours. Tammy found a tenderness and understanding in Silvie that she had never known from her husband.

She also found that her new girlfriend was very submissive, and with Tammy being a dominant personality, they made quite a pair. The two new lovers were soon getting together every time they got a chance and their love for each other grew. This kept Tammy's mind clear of Barker. For a little while, anyway.

Then on that terrible day Jack came home in a better than usual mood.

He was all excited about an idea that he came up with that would maybe finally be getting them the Tedford farm, a large property with an antebellum home on it that Jack wanted bad. He told her all about how he was going to use evidence from a 'dead nigger whore' to convict old Tom Tedford's son of murder and force his father to sell out.

"You might be fixing that old mansion up before long, before long at all!" he told Tammy as he walked up behind her, placed his arms around her and gave her a hug. Then he bragged in a cheerful voice. "And I only had to go down the road a little ways to get the whore!"

Tammy felt like somebody had kicked her in the stomach.

"R…Really, Hon?" she asked, even though she somehow knew the answer.

"It's that Tower girl." Reid answered as he took a sip of his beer. "You know, she lives on Blue Creek Road."

Within the week Reid's plan had played out. Silvie had been found dead in an abandoned house and Tommy Tedford had been arrested and charged with her murder.

This broke Tammy's heart and she swore she would get Reid for this somehow, someday.

And now, Daniel Barker was back! And he was so close she could actually reach out and touch him! And she *had* touched him, just a few minutes ago! Maybe he would be available this time. She wouldn't let this chance get away.

But now there was Jack. Jack would have to go. Yes. Jack *would* have to go. Maybe Pope could help. And then she would get rid of him, too. That would tie up a lot of loose ends.

"What kind of thoughts?" Tammy asked Jack, noticing the grin on his face.

"Old Barker might've come back home at a real good time." he said as he lit up a Marlboro. "We've got several pieces of land we need to move. It wouldn't be good to get caught with too much on hand if things ever go south. Cash would be easy to grab and take off with. He might be just what we need."

He's just what I need! Tammy thought.

"He might be!" She agreed, idly scanning the stores on Main Street as they drove by. "He just might be!" She chimed. "But be careful. He's seems like a smart fellow." *A lot smarter than you.* She thought to herself.

"I've always been careful, ain't I?" Jack asked. "It'll all work out."

"I'm sure it will." Tammy replied as she thought about how Barker felt against her in the restaurant. It brought back memories of the Christmas parade. She could almost taste that kiss.

Barker watched the Reids drive away from the restaurant as he got in his F150. His mind was full of thoughts about everything Sarge told him last night. There was a lot going on here and a lot of questions needed to be answered.

He drove over to Sarge's place and found him in his small woodworking shop putting the finishing touches on a bird house that resembled the courthouse on the town square. There were twelve more hanging around the shop that were patterned after churches, gas stations and other buildings around town and one that looked a lot like the White House in Washington.

"You build birdhouses?" Barker asked as he looked around.

"Yeah." Sarge answered, his attention focused on the job at hand. "It's therapeutic." He paused a moment, then asked "What do you do for therapy, Cap'n?"

"I don't need therapy." Barker lied. "I'm all squared away."

Sarge turned and gave his old C.O. a very serious look. "After all of the shit you and me seen over the years?" He turned back to the bird house. "We *all* need therapy."

Truer words were never spoken. Barker tried to stay busy with his hobbies too, such as gunsmithing, hunting, and driving over as much of North America as he could. And some of these helped him forget about things he had seen and done on the job, but sometimes old memories crept in no matter what you did…or didn't do.

You had to be careful with those memories. Men have been dealing with them as long as they have been going to war and a lot of warriors won the battles in the field but lost the war after they got home. Drugs and alcohol have often been thrown up to block them out, sometimes with a tragic end. Deep, dark depression will accompany the memories a lot of times and can lead good people on a journey of no return. Too often, Barker's old friend, Death, has been waiting in the wings when the memories won out.

Barker found out a long time ago that when the memories became too strong and he needed to exorcise them, a simple toast to comrades and enemies alike with a little good whiskey would sometimes allow them all to go their separate ways for a while.

Depression had also visited him from time to time but it always left before becoming a real problem. It probably had other old warriors to visit and didn't have time to hang around.

Barker picked up a log cabin bird house and looked it over. The workmanship was great. "What do you do with these?" he asked Sarge.

"I sell a lot of them at the little festivals they have around here." He answered without stopping his work. "If I get real bored, I'll load up my pickup and go set on the highway where Baker's gas station used to be and peddle a few. And if I *really* get bored, I take some of them out in the woods and hang them on tree limbs for the birds, sort of a no income housing thing."

Barker put the cabin back where he got it. "I've been thinking about this thing with Reid. Are you sure everybody in the county offices is in on it?"

Sarge turned around and smiled. "What if I showed you some proof of them tampering with the voting machines?"

"What kind of proof?" Barker asked.

Sarge sat the courthouse on the bench and slid off of his stool. He walked to a beat up, gray filing cabinet in the back corner of the shop and dug through the drawer next to the bottom. A few seconds later he handed Barker a thick file, sat on the stool and went back to work on the bird house.

Barker opened the file and started to leaf through it. It took a minute for him to figure out what he was looking at but soon he realized that Sarge had amassed a collection of death certificates and voter registration forms. The names were the same on both.

"You mean they're using dead people to stay in office?" Barker asked.

"Well, that's one way to stuff the electronic ballot boxes." Replied Sarge. "I'm sure I didn't find all of them, but my last count was about three hundred dead folks that weren't registered as dead folks at the state health department. Faye has them in a kind of stand by file in her office just in case they can't move enough live votes around with the machines."

"Three hundred." Barker mumbled. "That's a lot of votes in a county this small. Why hasn't somebody noticed the extra numbers? They still post the election results in the paper, don't they?"

"Yeah, but that's only numbers. And they only use some of them if they have to." Sarge nodded at the file." Faye can use just as few or as many as she needs to at any one polling place and not flood the results. A few dead folks voting *for* a person while she *loses* a few live votes against, that makes a big difference when it happens in all twelve precincts in the county. And some people *have* questioned her about the final count in the past but she has the records to make it look legit. Besides, it's expensive to have the votes re-counted and nobody wants to put up the money. And more new people are moving in and out all the time so it's getting harder to keep up with everybody. It's not like it was years ago when everybody knew everybody."

Barker thought about this. "I'm going to call Will and get him to look at this thing. If it's a sleeper and nobody knows about it, he might want to help us out."

Sarge nodded. "That would be nice. We could probably use some big time help on this. What about Old Antioch?"

Barker nodded. "I'm going to tell him about that, too. Any time somebody's hiding bodies, they're up to no good."

The sleeper Barker referred to was an illegal situation that, for one reason or another had avoided the attention of authorities. In this case it was a quiet county that started with small illegal dealings and moved on to bigger things slowly enough that nobody really noticed.

Barker called this the 'bullfrog syndrome'. When he was in high school his science teacher taught him that if you put a bullfrog into a

67

pan of hot water, he would find it uncomfortable and jump out. But, if you placed him in a cool pan of water and slowly heated it up, he would stay there until he was cooked alive. People sometimes find it easy to ignore small things and this conditions them to ignore something a little bigger, and then something bigger still, until finally everything's gone to hell and they don't understand how it got that bad. Adolf Hitler was a prime example of a pan of water slowly coming to a boil.

"Sarge?" Barker asked. "How did you get hold of these records? You didn't night op the courthouse, did you?"

"Naw." Sarge drawled. "I'm always going in there and getting survey maps and old records for that county history piece I write in the paper once a month. People don't notice if you don't try to take too much at one time."

"You write a newspaper column?" Barker asked.

Sarge nodded his head and smiled. "Yeah, but don't sound so impressed. I just write a little something for the Telegraph. More therapy, you know."

"Sounds like you need a lot of therapy."

Sarge's smile faded and he spoke in a serious tone. "Look Cap'n. You and me and them other guys did a lot of shit in Africa and down south too. Some of us did alright. Some of us, uh, *struggled* when we came back. Some of us need more therapy than the others. I need as much as I need and I'm not afraid to admit that." He hesitated. "Not anymore."

Then the old NCO turned and picked the bird house back up and started painting the details on the steps.

Barker stood and looked at his old friend for a while. He was right…about everything.

"Are you coming to the funeral home after while?" Barker asked.

"I'll be there with bells on!" Sarge answered cheerfully.

As Barker walked to his truck, he passed a small flower bed at the corner of Sarge's house. It had two huge old rose bushes in the back and different kinds of smaller, colorful flowers in the front. Something else caught Barker's eye and he stopped and looked back toward the shop. When he was sure Sarge couldn't see him, he knelt down.

Mixed in amongst the flowers were lots of small, white tomb stones about six inches tall. When Barker looked closer, he saw that each one had a name on it. There was also a birth date and some had dates of deaths as well. Sarge had been keeping up with everybody he had served with in his own way. Barker found his own among the others. He straightened up and looked down at the shrine. "Therapy." He muttered to himself.

Meeting Death

For The First Time

After leaving Sarge's place Barker headed over to Uncle Det's farm, eight miles out of town in the hills above the river bottom. Talking to Sarge made him think about something he had been meaning to share with somebody for a long time but that someone just hadn't come along yet.

Barker wasn't even sure he *could* tell anybody without being committed to a psyche ward.

Eight months after arriving in Africa on that first job, a young Barker, Sarge and the other advisers had put together a pretty good little army and had been taking the fight to the bad guys for a while. They were making a name for themselves and pushing a lot of the enemy back toward the borders, especially in the south.

Then one rainy afternoon on the side of a ridge above a peaceful little valley they were ambushed by a group of independent fighters that didn't bother to choose sides. They fought for anybody that would pay and fought against anybody who had anything they wanted. They were mean as the devil and loved what they did.

 This particular day they outnumbered Barker's force almost two to one as they attacked from the uphill side of the ridge. The initial contact was fast and fierce but the new army stood and fought, using the tactics they had been taught as well as any seasoned troops would.

 In a few short minutes the enemy force had split itself, one part retreating over the top of the ridge and the other part retreating down the ridge into the valley.

 Sarge's group immediately gave chase with his men to the ridge top and was able to pour devastating fire onto the enemy retreating below. The chase lasted two hours and was a great victory.

 Barker led his soldiers after the other pack which was slowed down crossing the small river that snaked its way through jungle growth along the near edge of the valley. This caused the ones in the rear to have to turn and fight while their fellow comrades made the crossing. The ones in the rear did this with every weapon at their disposal and fought fiercely. Any critter will do that when he's cornered.

As the battle raged with new intensity, a rocket propelled grenade struck the ground near Barker, killing two of his local soldiers. The concussion hit Barker with the force of a speeding truck and he was thrown several feet before landing among large rocks and tree roots..

He tried to stand but his body was so stunned and weak he could barely crawl. It seemed to take forever for him to pull himself into a sitting position at the bottom of a large tree.

He surveyed the area as best he could and saw that the battle was now moving across the river without him. He tried to call out but he couldn't make any sound loud enough to be heard over the gun fire. He tried to raise his right hand and found that it still held the AK-47 he started the battle with.

As he pulled the rifle onto his lap his ears began to ring and he felt darkness wash over him.

Sometime later, the young soldier became aware that he was still alive as he moved from total darkness to a semi-conscious state.

First there was the ringing in his ears. Then, as that faded he could hear birds and finally, water running. In the far distance he could hear an occasional rifle shot or grenade exploding.

Now the smells were coming through. They were familiar aromas such as fresh turned dirt that reminded him of the farm.

Then there were the odors of burned gun powder and spent ammunition. And blood. And death.

As his senses slowly came back to him, Barker felt the comfort of the rifle under his right hand. Slowly, his hand crept to the lower receiver and found that there was a magazine there but there was no way to know if it still had ammo in it. And the only way to find out was to take the magazine out, but to do that he would have to move and that could give away his position if anyone was watching.

He pried his eyes open to a thin slit and ever so slowly scanned the terrain he could see without moving his head.

It was an eerie sight.

The sun wasn't quiet down and the light was filled with shadows and smoke. Dead bodies littered the area and weapons and other gear lay scattered among them.

His ears began to ring and he closed his eyes and said a short prayer.

When the ringing once again ceased he again opened his eyes and slowly changed the magazine, exchanging it for a fully loaded one from the chest pouch.

At least now he had a loaded weapon and his upper body seemed to work even though he wasn't too sure about his legs.

Then, as he wiggled his feet, something moving near the river caught his attention.

He froze and stared intently. There it was again! Something was coming toward him!

It was zigzagging through the trees and stopping now and then. It was far enough away that Barker couldn't get a good look at it but it looked to be big, much bigger than a man.

Barker's fist was tight around the rifle's grip and his finger was curled around the trigger as this 'thing' worked its way closer.

As it got closer, he saw it stop at a dead soldier and wave something over the body before moving quickly and silently to the next one.

"What the hell is that?" Barker asked himself.

Then as this thing moved closer, the young soldier could not believe his eyes! This thing was cloaked in a black robe with a hood and he was holding a scythe! An antique grain harvesting tool with a long, glistening, silver blade!

Barker squeezed his eyes shut so tight that his ears began to ring again!

I...I must be seeing things! He thought. *This can't be real!*

He ever so slowly opened his eyes again, sure that this *thing* would not be there.

But it was!

By this time Barker had forgotten about the rifle across his lap. He was mesmerized by none other than Death, The Grim Reaper, at work in front of him.

As he watched, this apparition would glide from one body to another, where a wisp of smoke would rise. He would swing his great scythe, held in his skeleton-like hands, through this vapor and reap the soul. It was strangely beautiful and peaceful to watch as it glided smoothly around the rough battle field.

Then, as The Reaper got closer and started to take another soul, he suddenly stopped and stood frozen for a second before quickly turning his head to Barker, who was expecting to see a skull or some hideous face. But the young warrior was surprised to see only a calm darkness in the hood. No face, no eyes, nothing but an unbelievably deep, black darkness.

The Reaper slowly stood to his eight foot height, placed his scythe across his right shoulder and propped his bony left hand on his hip as he slid to Barker.

He seemed to glide across the ground and made no sound at all as he stopped a few feet in front of the wounded Soldier.

Barker felt absolutely no fear as he looked up at this magnificent being standing in front of him.

"Have you come for me now?" he calmly asked.

Death shook his head and pointed his bony hand in a slow arc around the battlefield.

"You came for them?" he asked.

He nodded his head, turned and went back to work.

As he watched the spectacle in front of him, the fierce ringing in Barker's ears returned and he felt faint. He squeezed his eyes tight as a pain racked his body and the heavy darkness washed over him once more.

Sometime later Barker woke with a start as an ammonia ampoule was crushed under his nose. It was now dark and a medic with an Australian accent was tending to him.

"There you go, mate!" he said as Barker. "We'll get you back to camp and you'll be good as new in a day or so."

Men were moving everywhere in the dark. Orders were being barked as weapons and gear were being gathered from the dead soldiers who no longer had any use for them.

Barker was soon on his feet and his men were ready to head to Sarge's camp on the other side of the ridge. Barker's men had run their quarry into the ground and pretty much wiped them out. They were now heavily loaded with the spoils of the battle and prepared to move out.

As Barker watched the men began to slowly trudge up the trail, he shined his flashlight around the area. There, sitting on a log with his legs crossed, his bony fingers laced together over his knee cap and his foot bouncing up and down, was The Reaper. He nodded to Barker and Barker nodded back.

"Are you looking for something, Commander?" one of his men asked.

Barker couldn't help but smile a little. "Naw. I've seen enough. For now." But he was somehow sure he would see his new friend again.

The Reaper did visit Barker from time to time when there was work to be done and over time, that had turned out to be quite often.

He kept this to himself all these years. Sometimes he wanted to tell somebody about his friend, Death, but how do you do that? Everybody would think you were crazy and that could cause real problems in his line of work.

Barker hadn't thought much about it for while but this trip home and hearing Sarge talk about his 'therapy' made it feel like he really needed to talk to somebody. But not just anybody. It had to be somebody special. Somebody who would understand. And it would have to be at the right time.

Going To See Uncle Det

Det still had twenty five head of Herford cattle to keep him busy and the old man was coming out of the pasture on his old Massey Ferguson tractor when Barker drove up. A big hound led the way.

"Get out and come on in." Det called out his southern welcome as he shut the machine off and started to climb down, his old injuries slowing him down.

Barker got out of his Ford and walked slowly toward the house to give Det time to catch up. "Isn't this Ranger?" Barker asked as he rubbed the dog's big ears.

"Yeah. Annie said he was getting restless and she was afraid he might start treeing the neighbor's cats there in town so she asked me to bring him out here with me. He can tree whatever he wants to out here. Ain't nobody gonna' give a rat's ass, 'cept maybe the rats!"

The old man put his hand on Barker's shoulder and gave it a squeeze as they walked toward the house. "Now, what brings you up here to see your old Uncle Det?"

Barker hesitated a second and Det noticed it.

"Trouble?" he asked simply.

Barker shrugged. "Don't know yet. Maybe."

Det watched him closely. "Is it something about Tommy Ray?"

"Don't know that either. Not yet." Barker looked at Det "What do you know about him?" Barker felt strange asking this but he had been gone so long that he just didn't know his favorite cousin any more.

"Come on in the house. I've got a coconut cake the Widow Thomas brought by yesterday. You know, I think she's got the hots for me." He said, postponing the subject for a minute or two.

Barker followed Det inside.

The ancient Barker family home was an old dog trot cabin made from huge virgin pine logs harvested when Douglas Barker bought and cleared the farm. Parts of it had been around since fifty years before the Civil War.

It was originally a one room cabin that eventually doubled in size by a twin being built twelve feet away. This gap between the two was closed in later on by joining the roof and floor. This left a wide hall, or 'dog trot', in the middle. This was later closed with a wall across the front and back.

The roof was steep and housed a pair of rooms upstairs that were occupied from time to time by young Barkers.

The house had always been heated with a huge rock fireplace on each end of the house and welcomed any visitor with the warm aroma of all those years of hardwood smoke.

The next room to be added was a large kitchen built across the back. This was the room Det led him to.

The center piece was a long table made of wide, clear, virgin pine planks built by Papa Barker, Det's grandfather and Barker's great-grandfather. It was worn smoother from years of family meals than any sandpaper could've ever made it.

The old table also had knife marks on the underside that were made when it was carried outside in the winter, the top turned over, and used to carve meat on when they killed and butchered a hog or a beef.

There was also a story in the family about Mama Barker using it for an operating table after Papa's Kentucky rifle didn't kill the bear that was breaking into the hog pen. Papa and the bear had a wrestling match and Papa lost, but not before carving the bruin up pretty good with his big knife. Mama took time to finish the bear off with an ax and used some of the animal's own fat to patch up Papa. She was a strong woman.

Ranger took a place on a rug near the stove as Det placed a couple of plates and forks on the table beside a tall, fine looking, homemade cake as he and his nephew took a seat.

Without saying a word, Barker cut both men a generous helping and took a bite.

"Mmm! I believe that widow *is* sweet on you."

Det grinned at his nephew. "She'd be crazy not to be."

Barker forked up another bite. "Tell me about Tommy Ray." He said flatly before taking the second sweet mouthful.

Det played with his cake for a second then laid the fork down. "I don't know if he was into anything bad." he started slowly." But there's a lot of bad crap going on around here."

Barker chewed the cake. "What kind of bad crap?"

Det shook his head. "That damn sheriff, for one thing. He's just a little too *greasy.* You know what I mean? And I know this poor ass county ain't paying him enough to live like he does. And his wife

83

don't work nowhere. All she does is spend money and screw his main deputy."

Det had Barker's undivided attention. It might all be gossip but it was a start.

"Tommy Ray got to hanging out down in The Bottoms, at The Six Pack." The old man continued.

The Six Pack was a beer joint just across the county line in Schooner Bottom, or The Bottoms, as the locals called it. It had been mean country down there since the beginning of time.

That part of Grenada County is a small corner that's cut off from the rest of it by Grenada Lake and backs up to White Oak County. Grenada County is wet, meaning that it's legal to sell alcohol, while White Oak County is Dry, or alcohol free. The Bottoms is a lawless area that Grenada County authorities try to ignore and White Oak County has no authority in.

"What was he doing down in that hell hole?" Barker asked.

Det shrugged. "Don't know, but I hear that Pope spends a lot of time down there, too. He's sort of set himself up as some kind of *godfather* or something. It's a long way from any law, except Pope, but he ain't nothing but a damned outlaw himself." Det grimaced as if the name left a bad taste in his mouth. "A goddamn bed of snakes is all that place is." He paused a second and sort of gathered his thoughts. "I heard there was a girl hanging around down there that Tommy Ray was kind of sweet on." He shot a glance at Barker as he reached for the fork. "And you know what kind of gals hang out down there."

Barker knew. Back in his day, there were a half dozen, small run down travel trailers scattered under some big pine trees behind The Six Pack that were used as parlors for the whores to ply their trade in. If the trailers were full up, the other 'ladies' would do their plying on a handy pickup tailgate or the ground behind the trailers. Sex was plentiful, cheap and dangerous.

Barker took another bite of cake and chewed as he listened to his uncle.

"Any idea who this girl is?" He asked.

Det leaned back and grinned as he nodded his head. "Yeah. I know. Lucy Waits."

Barker almost choked on the cake from the surprise.

"*Lucy Waits!?*" He asked. "Lucy's working the bottoms?" This was hard for Barker to believe because Lucy was one of the classiest, prettiest, and most popular girls in school. This was the last place he expected her to wind up. "How in the hell did that happen?"

"Well, she went off to college and got a degree in business or accounting or something like that." Det told. "Then she went to work at the bank and did pretty good for a few years. But the bank don't pay much so when this guy, uh, Timmy Wagner, came to town and opened up a finance company, one of those high interest places that loans money to anybody. Well, he sort of caught her eye."

"Now, he did a real good business for a few years and made a lot of money. He built himself a big house over by the golf course and drove nice cars all the time."

"Him and Lucy got to dating and he hired her away from the bank and made her a manager. Everything was going good for them, and then stories started circulating around about the two of them doing a lot of drugs and partying real hard. Then one day, out of the blue, the loan company closes up and Mr. Wagner ain't nowhere to be found. It seems he took all the money and ran out on Lucy and left her to fend for herself. Then the auditors show up and she's ass deep in trouble. Six months later she's dead broke and everybody's suing her and nobody here'll give her a job doing anything. Next thing you know, she's peddlin' pussy in The Bottoms." Det took a bite of cake.

"And you think Tommy Ray was going down there to see Lucy?"

Det shrugged. "I really don't know. I just heard a rumor but I never got a chance to talk to him about it."

"Anything else?" Barker asked.

"I don't know if this had anything to do with anything" Det continued. "But him and Harry Pope had a hell of a cuss fight in town a couple of weeks ago. It just sounds kind of fishy to me that they get into it and Tommy Ray winds up dead a few days later."

Barker leaned forward and took another bite of cake. "Hell! I'd like to cuss Pope out myself."

Det seemed to be looking out into space as he mumbled softly. "There's just a lot of shit going on around here and people seem to be happy to let it happen."

"What about Tommy Ray driving into the Schooner?" Barker asked. "You got any ideas on that?"

Det shook his head. "He didn't drive off that road. I was down there when they pulled his truck out. The cab of the truck was bent under both doors and on the bottom of both sides of the bed. And the frame was crammed full of mud. It got that way from sliding over the edge of the river bank slow. If he drove that truck off the road and into that river, it would have jumped that edge and wouldn't have touched the bottom of the truck. "

"You seem pretty sure of that." Barker said.

Det smiled. "I worked a few wrecks in my day, remember?"

The elder Barker had been a member of the Mississippi Highway Patrol for twenty years after returning home from World War Two and had shot on their rifle and pistol teams for a lot of those years. With his military and law enforcement experience, Det would know more about both wreck injuries and gunshot wounds than most anybody else around here.

Barker took a deep breath before he spoke. "Uncle Det, you know Tommy Ray was shot, right?" asked Barker.

Det shook his head. "I knew they seemed to get him out of the water and into that hearse in a hurry when nobody was around." Then he cut his eyes to Barker. "How did *you* know?"

"I sort of, uh, broke into the funeral home and had a look at him." Barker replied.

Det thought about this a minute. "So, Lenard's in on it, too. Son of a bitch! You got any ideas as to who might've done it?" There was a lot of hate in those old eyes. Det didn't have any children and he loved Tommy Ray like his own son.

Barker shook his head. "Naw, but me and Sarge are working on it."

"Sarge? You mean that bicycle ridin' retard?"

Barker nodded. "He's a good man, Uncle Det. I've been in a lot of tough spots with him and he always came through. Besides, he's the one that put me onto this."

Det nodded. "I know, I know. It's just he's so damn…well, you know. *Different!*"

Barker got up and put his plate in the sink. "Yeah, I know. We might need a good man with a good rifle before this is all over with. Can you still hit anything with that old Winchester?"

Det got up. "Why, hell yeah! Just call any time you need me!"

"I'll do it." Barker replied. "We're checking on some things right now but I'm going to see about getting some help from an old friend up in Washington. And I guess I'll ride down in The Bottoms and see what I can find out."

"You be damn careful." Det stated flatly. "There's some mean sons of bitches down there."

"Yeah, well, I'm a mean son of a bitch myself." Barker replied as he headed for the door.

Det walked his nephew out to his truck and they chatted a few minutes before Barker left. As he drove away Barker noticed his uncle in the mirror. He looked like an old man leaning on that walking stick, but there was still a lot of man there. And Barker wouldn't hesitate to call on him if help was needed.

Pope

As he drove back toward town, Barker was thinking about the people who might be involved in Tommy Ray's death. He needed to get closer to the sheriff and Tammy. That would be easy enough, especially Tammy. But he also needed to get close to Pope, and that was going to be a problem since they had hated each other since they were kids.

Pope's department vehicle was a gray Yukon with a blue light bar on top and graphics down the sides. Barker saw it parked in front of Branson's Hardware Store just off the square as he was returning to town. This looked like a good time to 'accidentally' run into him and Barker pulled up to the curb.

Branson's was an old time hardware store that had been in this building since the 1930s. When Barker walked in, the smell and look brought back a flood of memories.

Jim Branson was the third generation owner and was glad to see Barker. As they chatted, Harry Pope walked by with a ten foot piece of dog chain in his hand.

The chief deputy had taken care of himself over the years. He was muscular, well groomed and his uniform was neat and pressed. He even had the same high and tight haircut even though it had become a salt and pepper over the years.

Barker would've recognized Pope not only from his physical traits, but also from the way he carried himself. He still had that "Billy Bad Ass" bully stroll he had in school.

Pope gave Barker a hard look but didn't say a word. As he passed by, Barker decided to make him speak. "Pope, are you not going to offer your condolences?"

There were several customers within earshot and Pope stopped and turned around. He faked a surprise look and a big smile. "Barker? Danny Barker? Is that you?"

Barker extended his right hand, forcing the chief deputy to shake his hand.

"Yep. It's me. How've you been doing?" Barker didn't over do the smile.

Pope's bleached white teeth were clenched. "Pretty good. Still with Sheriff Reid, you know."

Barker nodded. "Yeah, I know." He nodded at the chain. "Gonna'…
tie up a dog?"

Pope looked at the chain and nodded. "Yeah. I'm getting' a new
coon hound. Probably going to pick him up any day now." He
pointed toward the cash register. "Well, I've got to be going. Ya'll
have a good funeral tomorrow."

Bastard! Barker thought as he watched him pay for the chain and
walk out the door. He didn't care any more for that man now than he
did all those years ago.

Jim Branson also watched Pope leave. "I'm a Christian man and
probably shouldn't think this…" He said to Barker. "But that is one
man that I would not miss if something happened to him."

"Something's going to happen to him." Barker muttered.

"What was that?" Branson asked.

"Oh, nothing. Just agreeing with you, Jim."

As Pope drove out of town, he checked his rear view mirror
constantly. If someone, such as Barker, followed him, he would deal
severely with them.

Pope never liked Barker, even in school. Maybe if he had played
football with him and Reid, things would have been different but he

just never was a team player, Pope recalled. Barker always had to be so damned independent.

Back in school Pope could bully just about anybody but he couldn't bully Daniel Barker. He pushed him around some but Barker always managed to come out on top somehow and left Pope looking like a fool. Pope thought about picking a fight with Barker and beating the hell out of him like he had others but something made him rethink this strategy. Maybe Pope was a little scared of him.

He tried to make Barker look like a fool one time in front of most of the high school but Barker played the game so well that Pope was the one that came away looking silly.

Barker was talking to some other not so popular students on the campus after lunch one day when Pope walked up and announced in a loud voice for everyone to hear that Barker and his friends weren't welcome in this area. It belonged to the jocks and was off limits to anybody outside their little circle. Barker showed no emotion and let Pope finish his speech before shrugging his shoulders and saying "If that makes you happy." Barker walked away with his head held high.

Pope was expecting anything but that and, without at least a snappy comeback, he felt like a fool just standing there.

Then three events later that same year bothered him still today.

The weekend after the campus incident, Harry Pope took his father's aluminum Jon boat and went fishing on Grenada Lake. A few minutes after unloading the boat, it began to take on water. Pope quickly motored back to the boat ramp and arrived before it sunk. As he approached, he saw Barker sitting on a concrete picnic table. After watching Pope pull the boat onto the concrete launching ramp, Barker got up, casually walked to his truck and drove away.

Pope seethed all the way home, knowing Barker had drilled holes in the boat. But once he got home, he couldn't find anything wrong with it.

A month later, Pope took his red bone coon hound, Birdie, to the Schooner Bottom Hunt, the biggest coon hunting competition in the area. Birdie was probably the best dog in the north part of the state and Pope was sure to win big.

When the big day arrived, the weather was cool and the ground was damp from a recent rain, making the conditions ideal for Birdie to strut her stuff. But, instead of blowing everybody out of the water, she refused to even trail a hot scent. When the scores were tallied she finished dead last, right behind a treeing walker that was hit by a truck and killed crossing a highway…while running a coon.

As Pope was loading Birdie into his truck to leave in disgrace, Barker walked by and said "Tough break." Pope had never seen him at one of these events before and was sure he was responsible for Birdies' poor performance. But how?

The last thing occurred one day in June. Pope had a hopped up 1973 Camaro he took to the drag races once in a while. That morning he drove it to Little Mountain Speedway and the sports car ran like never before. It felt as if an extra one hundred horsepower had been poured into the big V8.

But then, as he was getting ready to run the last race of the day, the big money race, the car began to smoke from both headers. Not just a little smoke, but thick, blue smoke made from large amounts of oil being pumped into the cylinders! This was oil that would not only contaminate the carefully metered fuel/air mixture but would also leave burned deposits on the spark plugs and valves causing the muscle car's engine to miss and lose power!

Pope's last race was a dismal failure! He lost by ten car lengths and he had bet his earlier winnings with some of the guys in the pits and lost that.

As he was driving the car toward the gate trailing a thick smoke trail behind, he noticed none other than Daniel Barker sitting in a lawn chair in the back of his Ford pickup watching the race. Barker looked at him and smiled as Pope drove by.

Harry Pope knew with all of his heart and soul that Barker had something to do with all of things but he could not figure out how. He finally began to think that maybe Barker knew some kind of Voodoo or other kind of witchcraft and had hexed him. The bully decided the best thing to do was stay away from Barker and see if his luck changed. It did.

But now Barker was not only back but he was buddying up to Reid. Pope and Reid had too much going on and Pope didn't want another partner, *any* partner, and especially Daniel Barker. Well, something would probably have to happen to Mr Barker! And as far as that goes, something might have to happen to Sheriff Reid, too. Jack had started to get careless and Pope did not like that.

And if he played his cards right, it just might look like Barker had something to do with something happening to Reid. Then Pope could take Barker out, all in the line of duty, of course!

"I think that'll work!" Pope said out loud. "Yep, I think that'll work!"

The Six Pack

"You're going *where?*" Sarge asked as he stood in his driveway talking to Barker through his truck window.

"Down to The Bottoms." He repeated. "I wanted to let you know in case I ran into trouble."

Sarge rubbed his jaw. "I don't know of a better place right off to run into it! Maybe I better go with you."

Barker shook his head. "Naw, I better go by myself. I'll play the part of a good old boy checking out the old haunts of his misspent youth."

"Well… if you think that's for the best. " Sarge replied with his hands on his hips. "You just be damn careful! There's a bunch of young thugs hangin' out down there that want to make a name for themselves."

As Barker started the truck he said "Sounds like Dodge City on a Saturday night at the end of a cattle drive."

"It ain't far off! About all that's missing is the stinkin' cows." Sarge replied.

 Mid-afternoon found Barker crossing the county line on a two lane county road full of pot holes. Here the old timber was starting to give way to old cotton fields that were cleared long years ago by hard men who were willing to fight the mosquitoes and cotton mouth water moccasins for the fertile land so they could eke out a living raising cotton for an uncertain market. This area was in the flood plain of the Schooner River so very few people lived here. Few witnesses and nearly no law combined to make this a very rough part of the world.

 The Six Pack was originally a rundown share cropper house that was on an old cotton farm owned by Bo Robert's grandfather.

  As a kid Bo seemed to stay in trouble and it got worse during his teenage years. He used up all the favors he could get from family and friends and wound up moving into this old falling down shack just to have a place to live.

 Bo stole a tarp off of a lumber truck and stretched it across the top to keep the rain out for the first year or so and heated it with a wood burning heater made from an oil drum. His décor was early

American redneck accented with bullet riddled road signs and pelts and horns from local animals. He eventually livened up the sagging front porch with a hornets' nest on a tree limb about the size of a five gallon bucket.

He ran a few trotlines in the lake and became proficient at catching catfish and buffalo. A hand painted sign across the front of the shack advertised fish for sale and he soon found that if he kept a case or two of cold beer around, he could make more money selling it than fish. The beer was a lot less work, too.

He sold bootleg beer for a while until somebody talked him into applying for a license from Grenada County to sell beer legally. Bo filled out an application, paid his fee and received his beer license in short order.

He wanted a catchy name for the place and put up a hand lettered sign offering a six pack of beer as the grand prize for the best entrant. Since the words "six pack" were the biggest and most legible ones on the plywood, somebody thought that should be the name of the place and The Six Pack was born.

Most of his clientele were from White Oak County because it was dry and this was the closest place to get beer.

As business grew, Bo knocked out the inside walls and installed a coin operated pool table and a longer bar. He lived in a small travel trailer he drug in because somebody had abandoned it on the side of the road with two flat tires.

But then, one warm summer night, the old beer joint's luck ran out. A fire broke out and it was soon a glowing pile of embers.

This was a setback but Bo had seen the light and soon had a concrete slab poured next to the pile of ashes and rusty nails.

The slab was built five feet high so when the lake water rose and flooded the roads and surrounding bottom land, as it does every year or so, he could keep the doors open and his customers could tie their boats up to the porch which stretched across the front. A cheap, green, windowless, metal building was erected on it and the new and improved Six Pack was in business.

There were only a half dozen pickup trucks in the gravel parking lot when Barker arrived. It was the middle of the day and the normal crowd would start rolling in closer to sundown. Most of last night's crowd probably hadn't got up yet.

Barker parked near the right corner of the building with a clear shot straight ahead to the road so if the need arose, he could leave in a hurry and wouldn't have to back up or maneuver around other vehicles.

As he walked up to the industrial type steel door, he couldn't help but notice more than a dozen bullet holes around the door and another eight in the door itself. Somebody had filled most of them with clear silicone caulk to either keep the fresh out or the smoky, stale air in.

As he stepped inside and the door closed behind him, Barker stopped and took a moment for his eyes to adjust to the dim interior. He was also bombarded by that true beer joint smell; a combination of old cigarette smoke, stale beer and piss.

An assortment of tables and chairs were scattered around, their only common thread being the dirty red and blue plastic ashtrays with beer company logos on them in the center of every table.

The mandatory coin-op pool table was straight ahead and eight patrons were gathered at the far end of it as the juke box belched out a loud country song.

To his right were five waist high beer coolers lined up with a beat up Formica top running the length of them to form a bar. An assortment of well worn bar stools were scattered across the front to provide seating. The main light source was a few neon beer lights hanging on the wall behind the bar.

As he took a seat on a handy stool a female voice called from the gathering of souls behind the pool table. "What can I get you, Sugar?"

Barker recognized her almost as soon as he saw her headed his way behind the bar.

"Well, hello Dolly!" he sang out.

She was in her early sixties but looked a lot older with her frizzy dyed hair, pale, wrinkled Marlboro skin with too much cheap makeup caked on and bad teeth.

Dolly looked hard at him. "Do I know you?"

"You did a long time ago." He answered. "I'm Daniel Barker."

"Daniel Barker! How the hell've you been doing?" she said loudly as she reached across the bar and slapped him on the arm the quickly added "Oh! I'm so sorry about Tommy Ray. He was a real sweetheart!"

Barker nodded. "I appreciate that." After ordering a beer he asked. "I thought you'd be out of here by now."

With a wave of her hand Dolly said "Aw, you know how it is! There ain't no retirement plans for old whores unless you find a man that'll fall in love with you and take you away from all this!. And I never did..." Her voice trailed off sadly. "What brings you down *here?*" She asked. "The last I heard anything about you was in a big newspaper article. Something about you *retiring* from the army, or something like that." She sat a long neck Budweiser on the counter without bothering to open it.

"I'm just riding around and checking out the old stomping grounds." He replied. "I hear an old friend of mine is working down here some."

"Yeah?" Dolly asked. "Who's that?"

"Lucy." Barker answered. "Is she still around?"

"Yeah, but she won't get here till sometime after dark." Dolly said as she lit up a cigarette. "Do you want to wait on her?"

"Naw, I don't guess." Barker answered. "I've got to get back for Tommy Ray's visitation at the funeral home." He thought for a second and pulled out his wallet. "Could you give her my card? I'm trying to touch base with some of the old friends while I'm in town."

Dolly took the card, read the front, turned it over to glance at the blank back and then stuffed it in her back pocked. "Sure. I'll see that she gets it."

Just then one of the customers at the back of the building called to her. "Hey Dolly! It's getting' lonely back here!"

"It was good to see you, Dolly." Barker said as she turned to head back to the party.

"You too, Danny." she replied. "Keep your pants on, at least till I get paid!" she yelled to the back, getting a few laughs.

As Barker nursed the beer, the door opened slowly, flooding the building with clean sun light, the beam cutting through the smoke and dust hanging in the air. He waited until the door closed before looking over his right shoulder to see who the new arrival might be.

The man stood there scanning the room before stepping away from the door. When his eyes got to Barker, he stopped and looked. "Ain't you Tommy Ray's cousin?" It was Bubba Tudor. Barker knew him a long time ago but Bubba was several years younger and they were never close.

"Hey Bubba!" Barker greeted him as he took a seat on a nearby barstool. "How's everything going for you?"

Bubba shook his head as he stretched across the bar and fished a beer out of the nearest cooler. He held it up so he could see the label, and after seeming satisfied with the brand, sat back down on the stool, screwing the top off.

"Hey, Dolly! I got me a beer!" he called out to the bar maid, who was wedged between two of the customers beside the pool table with her tee shirt pushed up over her saggy tits.

"OK, Bubba!" she yelled back from the middle of the sandwich.

"Things have sure been better!" Bubba said before he took a long swig. "You got an old lady?" He asked as the bottle left his lips.

Barker shook his head. He felt a long, sad tale coming.

"Well, I do! And she's crazy as a damn road lizard!" The young man began. "We fight *all* the damn time! I've tried to leave her, just move out and be done with it but when I go to get all my shit, she calls the law on me! Tells them that I'm beating up on her! What am I supposed to do? Huh? What am I supposed to do?"

"What do you *want* to do?" Barker asked quickly.

"Well, uh, I want to get my shit without goin' to jail!"

"Then go get it when she's not there." Barker advised.

"But she's there all the time it seems like! The bitch ain't got no job. She don't do nothin' but set around and eat Little Debbie cakes all day! I just want to be a free man to come and go as I please!" Bubba took another swig of beer.

"So…" drawled Barker. "You need to get her away from the house long enough to get your stuff loaded up and get away. Right?"

"That's exactly what I need to do." Bubba took another long swig. "You got any ideas?"

Barker rubbed his chin as if in deep thought. "Hmmm" he hummed, then slapped the bar. "I've got it!"

Bubba lit up. "What? What? Got what?"

Barker leaned forward and spoke in a low, excited tone. "This is what we'll do! You take off and go somewhere for a couple of days. Some place where nobody knows you like, oh, Jackson or Tupelo. Now don't tell *nobody* you're leaving. Not a soul or this won't work!"

"OK! OK!" Bubba's excitement was growing. "Then what?"

"Then after a couple of days I'll call, uh, what's her name?"

"Emily!"

"Emily! Yeah!" Barker was feeding the excitement. "I'll call Emily and tell her I'm the sheriff of, oh, maybe Tunica County. I'll say there's been an accident, a *terrible* accident and I need her to come over there right away to identify the body!"

Bubba was beginning to look confused. "Body? What Body?"

Barker leaned closer. "*Your* Body!"

Bubba seemed confused. "But…but I'll be in Jackson…or Tupelo! Won't I?"

"Yeah! Yeah! But she won't know that!" This was getting good!

"So I tell her about the accident, but not *too* much about it. Got to keep her curious, you know…"

Bubba's head bobbed up and down. "Yeah! I got it!"

"You and me'll park down the road" Barker went on. "And when she tears out of there to go to Tunica to identify *your* body that ain't there, we'll go up there and get your shit!" Then with even more enthusiasm he continued. "And, hey! Hey! While we're there we'll take *her* shit too! That way, when she gets back she'll think she's been robbed! Won't that be a hoot? And you can give her hell for letting your shit get stole!"

Bubba slowly rose to his feet and backed away from the stool. "Hell naw! It won't be a hoot!" he pointed a finger at Barker. "You...you son of a bitch! That's some mean shit you're talking about! You, you just stay away from her!" he backed to the door, turned and quickly stepped outside. "That's the woman I love you're talking about!"

"But, Bubba!" Barker whined. "Don't you want to be a free man and all? It'd be a hell of a joke on her and later on we could all get together and just laugh about it!"

"Fuck you!" Bubba called back angrily.

As the door started to swing closed Barker called out cheerfully "Tell her Danny says hey!"

"Fuck you again, you son of a bitch!" his voice fading with distance.

When the bar returned to its natural darkness, Barker picked up his beer. "Rednecks in love!" he muttered as he turned it up and finished it off before heading back to town.

Visitation

The sun was going down as Barker drove to the funeral home and parked on the square.

This place gives me the creeps. He thought as he looked at the big, two story funeral home. *Especially at night. In the dark. On the inside.*

The funeral home was a big, white, two story, wood frame house with a porch across the entire front and a carport on one end with a shiny, new, black Cadillac hearse parked in it.

It was once the finest home in town and was the residence of the town founder, E.H. Henderson, who was a timber and land tycoon at the turn of the twentieth century. He had it built on a corner of the town square which was the hub of activity but he had moved his family back to Memphis in the late forties when a post war boom hit the big city.

The house sat empty for several years until Lenard Morris got out of the army in 1953.

He set up shop on the lower floor of the old house and resided upstairs. While this practice was common among morticians, especially in the south, it didn't do much for Lenard's social life.

A few years later he went to a mortician's convention in Cincinnati Ohio and brought back a bride named Nancy who was just as weird as he was. They lived on the top floor while he plied his trade downstairs and eventually they had three daughters, April, May, and June, who were born in February, August and October. They carried on the family tradition of being weird, just like their parents. This was probably aggravated by growing up in a funeral home.

The building itself was really quite nice except for that one thing that screamed funeral home; the big, white, round clock with the blue neon light around it that was mounted on the center of the front porch roof. This one had a sign arched over the top that read 'Welcome to Morris and Sons Funeral Emporium' and across the bottom, 'We Treat Your Loved Ones Like They Are Our Very Own'. There never were any sons, only the three daughters, but when Lenard ordered the clock, the manufacturer made a mistake on the sign. Lenard was going to have to pay the shipping to send it back and have it corrected but he was too cheap so he just put it up like it was and lived with it all these years.

There was a good turnout for the visitation and Barker spoke to a lot of old friends and family that he hadn't seen for years. He also saw Lenard mingling with everybody.

The undertaker was a tall man, around six foot two or three, and lean, not an ounce of fat on him. His hair was slicked back with some kind of gel, shiny and black as the darkest night without a single gray showing anywhere.

His black custom tailored three piece suit fit him perfectly, the Windsor knot in his narrow, black silk tie was extraordinary and his Italian loafers wore the highest shine imaginable. He could probably use the shiny toes for mirrors and look up ladies' skirts as he carried on a conversation with them.

As he moved from person to person, his deep voice rolled out as smooth as the best Tennessee whiskey, just loud enough to be plainly understood but quiet enough as to not disturb the atmosphere.

He reminded Barker of John Carradine in one of the actor's classiest rolls.

Lenard Morris must have had a portrait of himself in the attic that aged just like Dorian Grey, because he looked exactly the same way he did before Barker joined the Army. But between Grecian formula to keep your hair unnaturally black and a readily available supply of corpse make up to maintain that youthful look, a man would only have to contend with keeping his weight down to look young forever.

Barker made it a point to speak with the undertaker and as he approached Lenard, Barker extended his hand.

"Lenard Morris!" Barker addressed the man. "I just wanted to let you know how much I appreciate everything you're doing for Aunt Annie."

"I'm just glad to do what I can during sad times such as these." Lenard replied in a well practiced tone as he handed Barker a business card as the handshake broke. "Please, keep me in mind for any future services I might provide for you and yours."

Barker smiled. "Everybody's a potential client, eh, Lenard?"

The undertaker smiled his best smile. "Nobody gets out of this world alive." He replied and then turned to work the crowd.

There wasn't any reason to keep an eye on him. He wasn't going to do anything here.

Barker found Aunt Annie standing at the head of Tommy Ray's casket and took a place beside her.

Sheriff Reid and Tammy arrived early. Reid put his arm around Aunt Annie and told her how sorry he was about Tommy Ray and he was there if she needed anything, *anything* at all.

Tammy wrapped her arms around Barker and ground herself into him like a horny octopus.

"Oh! Danny!" She cried tearfully. "I'm sooooo sorry about Tommy Ray. He was such a good person! We'll all miss him terribly!" She was quiet good at this. It probably had something to do with pretending to give a damn about the good people of White Oak County all these years.

"I, uh, appreciate that, Tammy." Barker said as he tried to break her grip and put a couple of inches between them as his eyes burned from her ever present perfume fog.

She held onto his arm and looked up at him with a smile and a little wink. She was about as subtle as a smack in the head with an ax handle.

115

"I need to talk to you some time when there aren't so many *people* around." She hissed to him in a whisper."

"Really?" Barker asked. "Anything interesting?"

"I'll *make* it interesting!" Tammy promised.

Barker looked at her and for a second he saw that cheerleader that kissed him before the parade. "Sounds…*interesting.*"

"Don't it, though?" She cooed.

Reid stepped up just then and shook his hand. He reminded Barker to let him know if he could help out in any way at all.

As the Reids walked away, Aunt Annie waved her hand in front of her face. "Boy! You smell like a two bit whore on Saturday night!" Aunt Annie wasn't one to mince words. "And I think *that* whore likes you." She added with a lot of sarcasm, looking in Tammy's direction. "But don't get too excited. I hear she likes a lot of people, if you know what I mean."

Barker placed his arm around his aunt's shoulder. "Yeah I know what you mean, Aunt Annie." He answered.

Annie patted Barker's arm as she nodded toward the Reids. "I don't know what you and those two are up to, but you be careful, Daniel Barker. I don't want to do another funeral any time soon."

He gave Annie a tight hug. "I'll be careful." Then, as he started to walk away he stopped. "And you'll be proud of me. I promise." He told her.

Barker walked through the stuffy, crowded interior on his way to the porch to get some fresh air. There he visited with some old friends in the cool, night air.

Stories were told about things such as the time several of the boys were sitting on the square late one night and heard a truck coming which turned out to be the local drunk, Sammy Walters. He drove around the square and waved at the boys before stopping and backing up to the curb in front of this very funeral home. There he got out and staggered to the back of the truck, noisily dropped the tailgate and dragged something out onto the manicured lawn before slamming the tailgate shut, getting back in and driving back around the square, waving at the boys again and heading toward home. The boys walked across the square wondering if he had left a dead body there like you would leave a book at the library after hours.

When they got there they saw that it wasn't a dead body, or a live one. It was the "We Give Quality Stamps" sign from the Piggly Wiggly store.

They also talked about the time that Barker and Tommy Ray got into trouble for skeet shooting a big box of stuffed animals that they had found at the fairgrounds after the carnival pulled out of town one fall. They took turns throwing them into the air while the other one shot the cheap toys with a twelve gauge shotgun. The only real problem was that they were blasting the stuffing out of the cute little bunnies and kittens and rabbits and whatever within sight of a day care around noon and the kids were watching them from the play ground. Parents reported problems such as nightmares and bed wettings for months.

As the sheriff and Tammy walked out of the funeral home, they approached Barker once again.

"We'll see you tomorrow for the funeral." Reid said as he shook hands with Barker. "We'll have ya'll a real nice escort set up for the trip to the cemetery."

"I appreciate that, Reid." Barker answered. "And I'm sure it'll mean a lot to Aunt Annie."

Then as Reid stepped away to speak with some voters, Tammy walked up and hugged him again, this time pressing her big fake tits harder against him and giving them a quick sideways wiggle.

"I really am so sorry about Tommy Ray, Danny. Really, I am." She brushed her lips against his cheek. "And I can't *wait* to talk to you…alone." Then she pulled back and took his hand in hers, pausing before turning it loose, and then followed Reid down the steps.

I bet. He thought to himself.

"That was really sweet!" Sarge said from behind Barker.

As Barker turned toward his old friend, his eyes scanned the immediate area before opening the hand Tammy held onto so sweetly and showed Sarge one of Lenard's business cards folded in half.

Sarge stepped closer and lowered his voice. "From her?"

"Yep." Barker stated as he unfolded it. Written on the back was 'Call me' and a phone number with a little heart on each side.

"What do you think that's about?" Sarge asked.

A smile slid across Barker's face. "A good looking woman leaves a note for a fine male specimen such as myself and you have to ask what it means?"

Sarge shook his head. "I know you ain't desperate enough that you need to mess with *that,* are you?"

"Not by a long shot!" Barker assured his old friend. "But if I do any *messing,* it'll be for the cause. I bet she's just full of information."

Sarge hung around until the visitation was over and everybody drifted away. It was a Wednesday night and the only traffic around the square was a lone vehicle passing through once in a while. They sat on the tailgate of Barker's truck and talked about old times for a while before turning in.

Day 3

The next morning was filled with funeral preparations. When eleven o'clock finally arrived friends and family gathered at Lenard's mortuary.

The funeral was in the chapel at the funeral home but in times past, they were held at the church. Nowadays it had become the custom to have them here and drive straight to the cemetery.

Lenard had converted a couple of rooms in the old house into a nice, large chapel with lots of dark woodwork and high ceilings.

Aunt Annie and her closest family were in the front row on the right side of the aisle and Barker and the other five pallbearers were on the front row on the left. A group of ladies from the First Baptist Church choir sang several old hymns before Preacher Adams took his place behind the podium.

He was a tall man with well groomed gray hair and a very nice black suit. He opened with a prayer and then, after another hymn, in his deep voice he started to praise Tommy Ray and his life on this earth.

The preacher told of the wonderful, obedient, child he had been and what a good student he was in school. He preached about Tommy

Ray being a fine young man and helping everyone he met in any way he could. He went on and on and on about all the great things Tommy Ray had done. He really poured it on thick and there wasn't a dry eye in the house...except one.

Barker listened for a while and began to get confused. He loved his cousin and Tommy Ray was a good person and all, but the preacher was making him sound like some kind of angel here on earth.

And Barker's memories weren't of an angel, earthly *or* heavenly. They were of a teenage boy who could steal the gas out the highway department tractors with a siphon hose and not get a single drop in his mouth. Or the guy who won a case of beer once in a while cutting cards with a marked up deck that he kept handy. And there was shop class in high school when Tommy Ray sanded two quarters down and soldered them together to make a two headed coin to cheat the junior high kids out of their lunch money. Hell! Half way through the ceremony, Barker was beginning to wonder if he was at the right funeral!

After the preacher finished up and another round of hymns, they loaded Tommy Ray's casket in the hearse and the procession of automobiles followed it to the cemetery led by the sheriff himself. It was a somber ride as was the grave side service but the fall day was clear and mild and people took their time leaving, some choosing to visit for quite a while.

Afterwards, a lot of people went back to Aunt Annie's and visited there. Barker hung around for an hour before calling Ried and a few minutes later they were headed east on Highway 12 in the sheriff's Tahoe.

"This place here," Reid said as he motioned to the left side of the road. "Is twenty four hundred acres and owned by an old bastard named Tom Tedford. It's his old family farm but he's just letting it run down. I offered him a hundred dollars an acre for it but he won't sell it…yet."

"You're not going into business against me, are you?" Barker asked as he looked across large, empty fields.

Reid laughed. "Naw, I want this place for myself. I've been trying to buy it for years and when I do, I'll call it White Oak Plantation. Tammy wants to redo the old house like one of those plantation mansions with big, white columns on the front and a balcony porch across the upstairs. We can have big parties and rent it out for cotillions and weddings and such. I'm going to plant food plots for the deer and turkey and raise some quail. I'm gonna flood some of the fields for the ducks and geese, too. Have me a real gentleman's club. I might even give you a discount on a membership."

Barker laughed. "That sure would be right nice of you, boss."

"You can forget that 'boss' shit." Reid replied. "We're going to be partners on this land thing, you know?"

Barker did the math on the Tedford place and said "That's two hundred and forty thousand dollars not counting all of that re-decorating you're talking about. That sounds kind of steep on a sheriff's salary."

Ried thumped the Marlboro butt out the window. "I've got it covered. Besides you and me are going make a bunch of money, right?"

"Sounds like you've got it all figured out." Barker replied.

"Yep. The only hold up is old man Tedford selling it or kicking the bucket." There was a lot of resentment in his voice.

"Does he have any kin folks that might have something to say about you getting the place?" Barker asked as he scanned the property as it rolled by.

The sheriff smiled a wicked smile. "Oh, he's got a boy, but I sent him to the pen a year or so ago."

"Just to get the land?" Barker asked a little surprised.

"Well..." He said with a little laugh. "The boy went and got himself convicted of killing a nigger whore. I've got a couple of friends over there at Parchman Prison who are going to, uh, 'talk' to him about his daddy's place."

"Damn, Ried. That's kind of severe, ain't it?" Barker asked as he watched the sheriff closely.

Ried shrugged. "Well, a man's gotta do what a man's gotta do."

Barker thought for a minute as they traveled down the empty highway.

"Is that place the only reason you brought me out here?"

"Naw, there's another place I want to show you up ahead." Ried said, pointing down the road.

They drove a few more miles before turning right onto a gravel driveway that was a collection of ruts and gullies washed out by the Mississippi rains and lack of maintenance. Reid had to zig zag to stay out of these washes and to keep from scraping his truck with the tree limbs that needed trimmed back on both sides.

"This drive way will need some work before we show it to anybody." Barker said as the truck bounced across a deep rut.

"No problem." Reid answered as he shut the truck off in front of the modest brick house and got out. "We'll just have the county road crew run a load of asphalt out here. They'll make it slick as glass."

"I thought it was against the law to use county supplies and equipment for private use." Grunted Barker.

Ried laughed. "Only if you get caught, my friend. Only if you get caught." Then after a little laugh he added. "You worry about *selling* the property. I'll worry about *getting* the property."

The farm they were on was four hundred and eighty acres with an older house that was well kept, a few equipment sheds, a barn and a couple of ponds that Barker could see across the cross fenced pastures, but it was clear that the yard hadn't been mowed for a while and nobody lived in the house.

"Why's it empty?" Barker asked.

Reid seemed happy to answer. "This place belongs to Ray and Jessie Anderson...or did. Ms Anderson went into a nursing home a couple of years ago. I guess she's got that Alzheimer's or something.

And Ray, well he drowned over on Grenada Lake three or four months back. He really enjoyed his fishing."

"Do they have any kids?"

"Not that I know of." Ried answered shaking his head. "Don't matter though. The taxes are past due and it's going to auction in a few months with all of the others." Then he winked at Barker. "But that's just a formality."

Barker looked at Ried. "I see. So if we want it we can get it?"

"Hell, boy! I get first pick of all of the delinquent tax property". Reid stated confidently. "The confiscated stuff, too. I got a safe full of really nice guns at the house that we've taken off of some of these rednecks around here. I'll show them to you sometime."

"I'd like that." Barker said smiling.

They walked around the Anderson place a few minutes, then Barker asked "Where's all of the equipment and cattle?"

"I'm sort of storing some of the tractors and stuff at my place and Harry Pope's got some of it at his. It would've just got vandalized or stolen if we had left it here."

"And the livestock?" Barker asked.

"Oh, we took the cattle over to Beechum's Sale barn in the delta and sold them for the Anderson's estate. I'm, uh, holding onto that money for them." Reid answered. "There wasn't anybody around to tend to them anyway, you know."

Barker made a mental note to remember Beechum's.

"You're all heart, Reid." He said to the sheriff.

Reid feigned humility with the wave of his hand. "Aw, shucks! Just a lowly public servant trying to help folks out!"

They walked around and talked about a couple of other farms that were available, one way or the other. The more Reid talked, the more he incriminated himself, and the more Barker let him talk.

Hanging the sheriff was going to be easy, but they were going to have to get some hard evidence somewhere to get the legal ball rolling. It wouldn't take much and then they could link other crimes to him and Pope.

It was still early when Ried dropped Barker off at the motel where he got in his Ford and drove up the highway to a pond where the sun was setting behind it. He got out and watched the sunset while he called Will Duncan.

Will offered his condolences for Tommy Ray and the two old warriors chatted for a couple of minutes before Barker told him what was going on with the bullet in Tommy Ray's head and the sheriff and his little gang.

"So...let me get this straight." Will said. "You went home for a funeral and found that there's voter fraud, murder, and no telling what all else is going on?"

"That's pretty much it, for now." Barker answered. "I just got here. I don't know what'll turn up tomorrow."

"This shouldn't be a problem." Will answered. "Especially with that bullet hole in your cousin's head. Will his mother let us exhume the body when the time comes?"

Barker took a deep breath and let it out slow. "I hope so. But we *are* talking about digging her only son up out of hallowed ground. Why don't we cross that bridge when we get to it?"

"That might be best." Will replied.

"There's one more thing." Barker added. "Sarge believes that the local undertaker is using an old church cemetery to hide bodies that need hiding."

Will was silent for a moment, long enough for Barker to ask "You still there?"

"Yeah…" Will drawled. "He hasn't, uh, *dug* anybody up, has he?"

"Not yet." Barker replied. "But he's probed a few and used ground penetrating radar on all of them. He has some pretty interesting theories. But the weird part is that if he's right, the undertaker is neck deep in something big."

"I'll have him checked out, too." Will answered as he took notes. "Have Sarge call me with a report on what he's got on this."

Since 9-11 Will's office had set up a huge bank of computers that allowed them to check on all kinds of information including taxes from the IRS, arrest and criminal records through NCIC, and travel records booked through the airlines.

"I'll get some people started on this tonight and I'll get back with you in the morning. " Will said. "We're open 24/7, you know."

Barker laughed. "Yeah, I heard that somewhere!" Then his tone got more serious. "How are we going to work this out? Don't we need some cooperation from the law down here?"

"Don't worry about that." Will answered. "I know somebody who knows somebody who knows a lot about the Governor down there. I don't think it'll be a problem. Know what I mean?"

Barker did know. Skeletons never stayed in the closet, especially when politics were involved. But while they *were* in there, it could be really handy to know about them.

After the call, Barker drove around the old, familiar country during that hour before dark. This was his favorite time of day and he had enjoyed it in a lot of places around the world under a lot of different circumstances.

He did a lot of thinking during this time, too. He knew if this thing was as big and crooked as Sarge believed it was, old friends and probably some of his family was going to be mixed up in it. That was the bad part about working here at home. It was always easier when he was some place where he was a total stranger.

And Sarge was going to be beside him in this until the end, he was sure of that. They hadn't talked about it but they didn't have to. And no matter how it ended, Sarge was going to be a hero to some and a traitor to others. Barker would get in his truck and go back to

Colorado and nobody would bother him. But Sarge would stay here.

This was his home.

Day 4

Early the next morning Barker got a call from the pentagon.

"Barker?" Will asked in a serious sounding voice. "What the hell have you two gotten into down there? Shifts changed out about an hour ago and intel is still rolling in on everybody on your list and people in all of the surrounding counties. You're going to need some help!"

"Is it that bad?" he asked.

"Yeah, it's pretty rough." Will answered seriously. "I'm going to have someone bring you a pile of papers to look over. He'll meet you out in the boonies somewhere later today. Will that work?"

"Yeah. Have him give me a call." Barker said. "It seems kind of quiet down here right now." There was a pause. "We're not jumping the gun, are we?"

There was a moment of silence. "Barker, you're not wanting to back out, are you? I understand with that being home and all. I could send somebody down there to run this job and you could go back to Colorado."

133

"Hell no! This is my baby!" Barker answered without hesitation. "I've thought about who might get caught up in it but it's got to be done. And I want this to be done right!"

"Alright then." Will replied. He changed the subject. "What we've got so far is a sheriff, chief deputy, and *every* elected official in White Oak County spending a lot more money than they are making. Sheriff Reid showed on his taxes that he made a grand total of sixty two thousand dollars, but he sold over ninety seven thousand dollars worth of cars, trucks and boats at Tilden Auto Auction in Pontotoc last year. That's not counting land and houses that passed through his fingers."

"Sounds like he does a little trading." Barker said.

"But he didn't show anywhere that he bought this stuff." Will replied. "Nobody does that kind of business legitimately without writing everything off his taxes that he can. And that's just the start. He and his wife have their name on some very questionable real estate in Memphis that they bought up over the last ten years."

"Memphis?" Barker asked. "Does it have anything to do with Ray Gantz?"

"Do you know him?" Will asked.

134

"Everybody around here knows him." Barker replied. "He's the titty bar king of the south. Everything from Memphis to the gulf coast. He's supposed to have his fingers in a lot of stuff. How's he tied in with Reid?"

Will hesitated a minute as he looked over some notes. "Your friend Reid owns several lots and run down houses that join property that some of Gantz's topless clubs are on. If Gantz has problems getting the permits he needs when he wants to expand, Reid could get them in *his* name on *his* property, as a sort of silent partner. It looks like they've done this in the past. That's something we'll probably be able to use later against both of them."

"Then there're the missing persons reports from down there. When Reid took office there were two unsolved missing persons reports on file anywhere that involved White Oak County Mississippi. Since he's been sheriff, there's been a bunch. It looks like there are eighteen or so on NCIC right now. The main one is a man, his wife and their two kids from Saint Louis who went to Florida for a vacation with some relatives during spring break this year. This guy has a younger sister going to college at Ole Miss there in Oxford and they were going to go by and see her on their way home but they never made it and nobody's seen them since. The last info on them is their debit card paid for gas at a Jiffy Quick gas station in Hendersonville."

"It's only about forty miles from here to Oxford." Barker said. "Nothing turned up?"

"Not a thing." Will stated flatly. "And you would think a green 1979 Chevrolet Caprice station wagon in mint condition would be hard to hide."

"A what?" Barker asked.

"A green 1979 Chevy Caprice station wagon that was supposed to be real nice. The guy was into restoring old cars and he was supposed to be good at it. He owned a shop in Saint Louis."

"That's one thing that I haven't seen around here. So this little job is a go?" Barker asked.

Will started slowly. "Not just yet. If you and Sarge could convince this Lenard Morris to, uh, *confess* to some of whatever he may have done with the bodies, that might keep us from being investigated too deeply after this is all over with. We still need a really legitimate reason for doing what we're going to do, you know."

Barker smiled. "I think we can handle that."

"We've got crews ready to send your way as soon as we get something." Will assured him. "We've already located a farm just off I-55 that was confiscated by the DEA. We can use it for a base."

Barker understood. "Give me and Sarge a little time and we'll make something happen."

Will laughed. "I'm sure you will. I'm sending a man down there with a pile of papers about your quiet little county. It makes for some interesting reading."

"I'm looking forward to it." Barker replied.

"Oh! And one more thing." Will had some concern in his voice. "Watch out for the sheriff and his old lady *and* that chief deputy. Watch your six."

"I always do, old friend. I always do." Barker answered before hanging up.

Later that morning Barker got a call from Agent Barry Watson, one of Will's up and coming men. He was still young and green but he was the one Will had picked to deliver some very important mail and that carried a lot of weight with Barker.

It was decided that they would meet at a cotton gin on Highway 430. There was going to be a farm equipment auction there in a week and a lot of tractors, combines and other used implements were parked around the yard. If anybody saw them there it probably wouldn't raise any suspicion, since they would think they were checking out the yard for deals on the day of auction.

"Mr Barker?" The young agent asked as he got out of his truck. The tall, blonde haired college boy type was wearing standard "special agent" attire; dark shades, black pants, black shoes, black tie and white shirt.

"That's me." Barker answered.

Blondie approached with his right hand out and his left clutching a stack of manila envelopes, all which bulged with papers.

"I'm glad to meet you. I'm Barry Watson. We spoke on the phone earlier." He pumped Barker's hand in a way that made him wonder if Barry would ever turn lose.

Barker smiled and pulled his hand free. "I'm glad to meet you, too, Barry. Is, uh, that for me?" he asked, nodding at the envelopes.

Barry was suddenly flustered. "Oh! Yes, sir! Sorry." He thrust the package at Barker.

Barker turned to use his truck hood as a table, keeping an eye on the nervous G-man.

"Settle down, Barry." He said smiling a little. "We're on the same side here."

Barry wiped his sweaty hands on his pants. "Yes sir. I know. It's just that, well, this is my first big field mission and I want everything to go well."

"Job." Barker said flatly while looking over the first page.

"Sir?"

"Job." Barker repeated. "Not a mission. Astronauts and pilots fly missions. We ain't astronauts."

"Right, Sir. Job." Barry said nervously.

"And I can just about guarantee you one thing." The older CGE continued. "*Everything* will not go well. Hopefully, enough things *will* go right that we will win and they will lose but everything will not go well. So don't be too disappointed when something goes to hell. Just learn from it and charge on."

One thing that Barker found on the first page was that, according to a contact at Parchman Penitentiary, Tommy Tedford was probably going to be in for a world of hurt if he stayed there. Plans were already in motion to pull him out with a bogus warrant charging him with theft of military goods while he worked a construction job on

Columbus Air Force Base near the Alabama state line. He would be transferred to the federal pen in Atlanta and placed in a secure section there. Barker made a mental note to see about getting Mr Tedford out of Hendersonville, too.

When Barker read all he wanted for the time being, he turned and faced the young agent, who was waiting patiently.

"Any surprises?" he asked.

"Uh, surprises, Sir?" Barry had been caught off guard.

Barker had to grin. *Damn. This kid's already squirming and I ain't even started cussing yet.*

"Yeah, surprises. Will just loves sending me surprises."

Barry stood still as a rock for a moment before answering.

"I... guess I'm it." He said in a weak voice.

This time Barker was caught off guard. He studied Barry before asking simply "What?"

Barry cleared his throat. "Mr Duncan said that I was to be yours to use in any way you wished for the entirety of this mission... I...I mean job."

Barker looked the young agent over slowly. "He makes you sound like a cheap whore, don't he?" He tucked the papers back into the envelope.

Barker was soon heading back to Hendersonville. Barry would show up there later and pose as Barker's hired hand in the land business. Barker told him to be sure and wear something that wouldn't stand out like his G-Man suit. Barry would get quite the education in the near future.

While Barker was making new friends, Sheriff Reid was conducting a little personal business on the sidewalk in front of the courthouse with Curtis Bellow, one of the local no-goods. The discussion was about the shipping of a couple hundred pounds of marijuana from the Bellow farm up in the hills to Memphis. A car horn drew Reid's attention to the street behind him, and as he turned, he saw Harry Pope pulling into the parking place beside his own pickup. "I'll come by your place later and we'll finish this up." Reid told Curtis.

"Just don't take too damn long." Curtis answered through the thick beard and moustache. "Me and the boys would hate for you to get to thinking' about it and back out."

Reid gave him a reassuring smile. "I ain't ever back out on anything before, now, have I?"

"I reckon not." Curtis answered as he shot a mean glance toward Pope. "We'll be waitin' on you."

Pope made no effort to get out so Reid started walking to him.

"What's that inbred son of a bitch want?" Pope asked nodding toward Curtis.

"Just asking for some farm advice." Reid answered." What do you need, Pope?"

The Bellow family had a hog farm about fifteen miles north of town in the hills that Dolton Bellows started in the 1930s. The family had lived on that ridge ever since and it was rumored that they made a lot of money since the beginning with pork, moonshine and, for the last ten or fifteen years, some of the best pot in the state. The remote area they called home was just about perfect for these things.

"We need to talk, Boss." Pope said flatly.

Reid smiled his best practiced smile. "What's wrong now, Harry? Did they run out of donuts over at the coffee shop again?"

Pope was not amused. "It's Barker. I don't think he needs to hang around here too long."

Reid dropped his voice. "You ain't getting a little jealous, are you?"

"I ain't jealous of that son of a bitch!" Pope spat. "You just seem to have pulled him in awful close awful quick. If he don't see it like we do, he can really screw things up for us!"

"You just let me worry about that." Reid answered quickly.

Pope pointed a finger at his boss. "I'm telling you! You better not fuck this…"

Reid's smile disappeared as he cut Pope off. "And I'm telling you, asshole, I'm the boss here and you'll do what I say and like it. Understand? Now, I can't afford to fire you because you know way too much. But there are other ways to *terminate* a problem employee. Understand?"

Pope hated being talked to like this but there wasn't much he could do about it. He might have stepped out of line but he knew that the only way he could get out of this partnership with Reid was if one of them died or disappeared. And he had been thinking about the sheriff doing one or the other a lot lately.

"Now get your ass out on that road and find something to do." Reid ordered.

"Yes sir!" Pope answered in a smartass tone as he put his truck in reverse.

Reid stood there with his hands on his hips watching Pope turn off the square. He thought about getting rid of his chief deputy a lot lately, too.

Reid knew Tammy had been screwing Pope since high school and it was worth a lot to have the deputy keep her busy while he was off somewhere screwing one of his girlfriends but lately Pope seemed to be trying to run things more and more. Maybe with Barker back in town, he could use his old school mate some how to get rid of his chief deputy. Of course, Barker would probably have to disappear, too…if everything worked out right. And with Tammy getting all hot and horny at just the mention of Barker, it might work out that she could wind up out of the picture, too. That would leave Reid with nobody to have to share his toys with. He smiled when he thought about it.

Lenard Goes For a Ride

Barker drove to Sarge's and found his old friend burning a pile of fresh raked leaves in his gravel driveway.

"What brings you out this way this time of the day?" Sarge asked as Barker stepped out of his truck and leaned against the side of the bed.

"Well..." Barker drawled. "I spoke with Will a while ago and he seems to think we need to see if we can convince Lenard to open up that warped brain of his and share the knowledge with us."

Sarge's head slowly turned and faced Barker. "He did what?" He asked slowly.

Sarge grinned like a little kid as Barker told of the plan to get the information they needed out of the old mortician.

"This'll be more fun than taking Big Wanda to a double feature at the drive in!" Sarge said as he rubbed his hands together.

"Just remember." Barker warned. "He has to be able to talk. We can't hurt him too bad and we sure as hell can't kill him!"

Nodding his head, Sarge answered, "Yeah, yeah! I hear you. But I can get his attention, *right?"*

Barker had to smile. "Right. I'm thinking that maybe we take him up to Old Antioch and lay out his choices. The atmosphere might play in our favor."

Sarge nodded enthusiastically. "How about I go over to the funeral home and act like I'm there to buy a bottle of whiskey and make him go with me. He won't suspect a thing!"

"That might work." Barker answered, rubbing his chin. "Can you get him to drive you up there in his hearse? I'll park close by and follow ya'll in my truck." He patted the top of the bed.

Sarge nodded. "I'm sure I can. Can I pull a gun on him?"

"I don't care what you do, as long as you and him come out of that garage in that black Cadillac." answered Barker.

Sarge asked with a gleam in his eye, "When do we do this?"

Barker smiled. As soon as possible."

146

Sarge reached for the door handle on the truck. "Let's go!"

Ten minutes later Barker pulled over and let Sarge out on the street behind the funeral home and then drove to the square where he could watch the front without drawing too much attention to himself.

As soon as he pulled over he watched Sarge casually stride down the side walk and into the front door of Morris and Sons Funeral Emporium. Ten minutes later the door on the attached garage slowly slid up and a shiny, black hearse pulled onto the street, the door closing behind it.

As the Caddy passed his position, Barker expected to see Lenard behind the wheel. He was mildly surprised to see Sarge driving and Lenard nowhere in sight.

"What the hell?" he muttered to himself, as he pulled in behind the hearse.

Barker pulled out his cell phone and punched a number.

"This is Mike Long. What can I do for you?" Sarge answered in a generic tone.

"Where the hell is Lenard?" Barker asked as calmly as he could.

"Oh! Hi Captain!" Sarge answered cheerfully. "He really didn't want to come along so I had to urge him a little."

"*Where is he?*" Barker asked through clenched teeth.

"He's in the back." Sarge answered flatly.

Barker mashed the gas and closed the gap between his Ford and the Caddy. Between the black curtains on the back door, he saw a copper colored casket.

"Is he in that box?" he asked.

Sarge's voice was as cheerful as ever. "Of course he is!"

"Of course he is!" Barker repeated.

Barker backed off and watched what little traffic there was for anybody who might appear suspicious. Twenty minutes later the two vehicles arrived at the ancient cemetery without incident.

As Sarge stood beside the hearse lazily stretching, Barker asked. "So… what went wrong back at the funeral home?"

"Nothing, really. It's just that, well, Lenard didn't want to do it our way, so I just sort of, uh, *improvised.*" The grinning soldier answered.

"Improvised." Barked stated flatly.

"Yeah! See, I told him that he needed to take a ride with me and he said 'Hell No! I ain't goin' nowhere with you!' and I said hell yes you are and he said hell no I ain't so I stuck my pistol to his head

148

and said if you don't get in that damn casket right there I'm gonna blow your damn head off and he said OK. Then I rolled it out to the hearse and loaded him up. Did I leave out the part about the casket being on a dolly?"

"I got that from you rolling him out to the hearse." Barker replied as he stepped to the rear of the bone wagon and reached for the chrome door handle. "Is there enough air in there to keep him alive until now?" He asked as he pulled the door open.

"Let's find out." Sarge answered as he reached in with both hands and pulled the casket out, letting it fall to the ground.

Barker's eyes followed it to the ground then cut back up to his old friend.

"Damn, boy!" he said laughing. "*That* ought to get his attention, if it didn't kill him!"

Barker stood back as Sarge bent down and unlocked the lid, then swung it open. There looking up at them was Lenard Morris; wild eyed, hair disheveled and his nice suit a wad of wrinkles.

"W…w…what do you want with me…" Lenard's eyes fixed on Barker as a surprised look crossed his face. "Daniel Barker?" He quickly glanced to Sarge, then back to Barker.

"Look! I…I…" he stammered as the casket lid suddenly fell shut in his face.

Sarge took a seat on it and looked across the old cemetery.

"Maybe he needs to think about whose out here for a few minutes." Sarge muttered.

"You're probably right." Barker agreed as he strode to back of his truck, dropped the tailgate and took a seat on it."Too bad it's not July or August."

Sarge nodded slowly. "Yeah. That would make it hotter'n hell in there right quick."

Muffled sounds began to come from the casket and it began to bounce around a little. It seemed that Lenard wasn't too happy being on that side of his business. After a few minutes he settled down and became quiet.

Another five minutes passed before it was decided to open the box again. This time, as Sarge raised the lid, the undertaker made a mad dash for freedom. It was a good idea but came to a sudden halt as his big nose ran head on into Barker's fist, knocking him out cold. His legs never cleared the casket as his upper body slumped onto the ground.

"D…damn!" Sarge stuttered. "You knocked the piss out of him!"

Barker shook his hand with the fingers outstretched. "Yeah I did. But I probably should've used a shovel."

"Can I hit him next time?" Sarge asked anxiously.

"Be my guess!"

The two old soldiers sat on the tail gate of Barker's truck and watched Lenard as he began to come around. First he moaned and moved just a little bit. Then, as his senses came back to him, he jerked upright, froze for a second, then tried that mad dash again. And he might have made it, too, if his right wrist hadn't been handcuffed to the box he was delivered in. This jerked him to the ground but he quickly jumped back up, grabbed the pall bearer handle he was cuffed to and tried to make another run for it.

"How far do you think he'll drag that casket?" Sarge asked lazily.

Barker shrugged. "Probably about twenty feet. That's how long that chain is that's got it hooked to the hearse."

When the slack came out of the chain and Lenard found that he couldn't drag the hearse too, he fell to his knees, a look of fear and defeat on his face.

"He's persistent, ain't he?" Sarge asked.

151

"Yeah, he is." Barker answered as he got up and walked to Lenard. "Time for the fun and games."

The undertaker looked like a cornered animal, on his knees on the ground, his face full of fear and his brain unable to comprehend the way his world had suddenly turned upside down.

"Wh...what do you want with me? I...I don't know anything!" He was almost crying.

"What happened to Tommy Ray Barker?" The question was simple.

Lenard shook his head rapidly. "I, uh, don't know what you mean!" He attempted to smile.

"Wrong answer." Barker shot back as he kicked Lenard in the chest, knocking the breath out of him.

Lenard fell, spun around and tried to scramble away, but the cuff and everything it was hooked to prevented anything but a very short escape. "What happened to Tommy Ray?" he repeated. This time, Lenard's brain scream at his to tell Barker anything, *everything*, but it also screamed loud and long about what would happen to him if he did.

Barker stepped closed and stated flatly, "This is the last time I ask nice..."

Lenard struggled to face the old soldier. "You don't understand!" He said through labored breathing. "I...I can't say anything! They...they'll kill me! And my family!"

Barker's face held absolutely no emotion. "So it's better that *they* killed *my* family? My cousin?" He shook his head slowly as he knelt on one knee. "I'm not going to kill you, but I will beat the hell out of you and then put your sorry ass back in that box and bury you in one of these stacked up graves you've got going on up here." Barker let this soak in for a minute. Lenard's eyes flew wide open when he realized that Barker knew about that. "Now, how long will you last in there, Lenard? Did you ever think about that?"

Barker's face was like granite. He didn't move. He didn't sweat. He didn't even seem to be breathing.

The same couldn't be said about Lenard. A new fear crawled across his face as he shot a glanced over at the cemetery then looked back at Barker as he began to shake violently.

Something flashed in Lenard's eyes and Barker saw it. The old soldier's eyes narrowed as he slowly turned his head and looked at the peaceful, hallowed ground filled with shady tombstones.

He took in this scene in for several long seconds before slowly turning back to Lenard. This time it was Lenard that saw something in Barker's eyes and it scared him so bad that he pissed in his pants.

Barker's voice was cold and low. "You buried these people alive!"

"N…no!" Lenard screamed as Barker's eyes burned into his very soul. "No! I…I didn't! Not all of them" Tears ran down his face as he began to weep uncontrollably.

"Not *all* of them?" Sarge's voice was barely audible and came from near Barker's right shoulder.

"That's what the man said." Barker muttered, giving him a long look before asking "How many people have you buried out here?"

"I, uh, I'm not sure." His voice was shaking.

Sarge stepped forward. "Why don't you give it a little thought?"

Lenard's eyes shot left and right and he started to count on his fingers. A few minutes he came up with a number. "15." he said.

"15?" Barker asked. "Are you sure?"

Lenard nodded his head.

Barker looked at Sarge. "Looks like you miscounted, old buddy."

"I don't think so, Captain." He drawled. "That's state of the art equipment I was using."

Barker thought for a minute, then looked at Lenard. "How many caskets did you put in the ground?"

"14." He quickly answered.

Sarge leaned back with a smirk on his face and extended his hands, palms up. "See? I didn't screw up!" Then the smirk slid from his face. "Wait a minute! Fourteen caskets and fifteen bodies? Then you put two bodies in one casket?"

Lenard lowered his head and nodded.

"That's cold, Grave Digger." Barker said. He suddenly felt a need to be alone.

Barker turned and walked to the cemetery. There, he stood in the cool shade of the

cedars and listened to the breeze blowing through the foliage. As he turned and looked at the newer graves scattered among the old ones, Barker wondered what awful hell some of these people went through here and what hell the rest went through somewhere before their dead bodies were deposited here. He knew he would find out, he had to, but all of a sudden he didn't want to.

In war zones Barker had seen some of the terrible atrocities that humans can inflict on one another. He saw the ditches full of soldiers who had been hacked to death with machetes because prisoners were too much trouble and sharpening a blade was cheaper than buying bullets. He had seen the villagers that had died after two or three days of torture before they were herded into a corral of brush which was set on fire and slow roasted them to death. He had seen a school bus full of elementary school children pushed off a mountain road because their parents voted for the wrong dictator in the last election.

The old warrior had seen a lot. He expected to see such things in the war torn lands he had served in, but never, not in his wildest dreams, had he ever expected to see anything like this. Not *here.*

This ground was set aside as a final resting place, a *peaceful* resting place, for the internment of those buried here to lie until the end of time. This was a special place. A Holy place.

But, now Lenard Morris and no telling who else had taken it upon themselves to come here and turn it into, not only a dumping ground for unwanted bodies of foul play, but a place to be used by evil men with evil intentions. Human beings had been brought here and subjected to unimaginable terror that could only be escaped by death.

Not a quick, maybe painless death, but a long, lingering death. A death that couldn't be hastened by the condemned but would have to be endured with no chance of reprieve. A death that would only come after the oxygen in the coffin ran out.

A strong breeze blew through the tombstones and Barker looked to his left. There, standing tall and still among the dead, was his old friend, The Grim Reaper.

His featureless face was turned straight to Barker and his scythe was resting in his arms. He was as still as any statue, only his robe moved a little in the breeze.

He had a job to do here, the same as anywhere else he went. Mr Death didn't have an opinion on anyone, good or bad, young or old. His only purpose was to reap the souls and deliver them to the Seat of Judgment. There was no compassion in him, no hate, no love, no emotion of any kind. Barker wished he could be like that.

As he turned and started back toward Lenard, Barker stopped. He looked back again at the tombstones and Death, who nodded before turning and fading into the forest.

Barker's next question rang out before he got back to the undertaker. "What's it going to be, Lenard?" His voice was hard. "In the box below ground or out of the box telling us everything about everybody. That's the only choices you have."

Lenard had been caught off guard and his voice was weak.. "I…I, don't know."

"Wrong answer!" Sarge sang out as he grabbed Lenard's arm. "Get in the box!"

Lenard started to struggle feebly. "No! Wait! I'll talk!" Then his body sagged and his voice fell to a whisper. "I'll tell you everything."

"Who did you bury up here, Lenard?" Barker asked impatiently.

"I, uh, I don't know all of them…"

"Who does?" Sarge followed up.

"I don't know! I Mean, I've got..I've got records on everybody…" Lenard mumbled.

Sarge shot Barker a quick glance. "What *kind* of records?" He asked.

Lenard sounded very tired. "I set up some cameras whenever they came in with somebody. I've got it all on disks."

"Where are these disks?" asked Barker.

Lenard drew in a deep breath and exhaled. "In the funeral home."

"Where in the funeral home?" Barker's questions came fast.

Lenard looked at Sarge. "Do you know that old freezer beside the back door?"

"Yeah." Sarge answered as he shot a glance at Barker. "It's under that window I climbed through the other night."

Lenard looked at Barker then back at Sarge with a confused look on his face. "You went into my funeral home at *night?"*

Barker leaned close. "Yeah. Now, about that freezer…"

"Slide it away from the wall." He paused again. "There's a box built into the floor. It contains everything you'll need…and more."

Barker and Sarge stepped away from Lenard.

"Do you want to go check that box out?" Asked Sarge.

"We need to get to it pretty quick." Barker answered. "When his buddies find out he's gone, it may get hard to get back in there. But we have to find something to do with Lenard until Will's people get here and they can lock him up."

Sarge snapped his fingers. "I've got it! Why don't we take him over to Grandpa's old place? There's that old armored car body buried in the hill in the pasture he used to use for a storm house. It's as secure as any jail cell."

Barker looked back at Lenard as he thought about this. "That'll work. I'll take him over there while you ease back into town and put that hearse back in the funeral home. Get whatever Lenard's got hidden under that freezer and slip out of there."

"I'll call you as soon as I can and let you know how it's going." Sarge said.

Barker and Sarge cuffed Lenard and put him in Barker's Ford and put the casket back in the hearse. A few minutes later they were off the ridge and driving in opposite directions.

A half hour later Barker had Lenard locked up tight in the bullet proof bunker. He left the captive a bottle of water and the promise that he would come back after they recovered whatever was at the funeral home and take him somewhere else or he would come back and show him a world of hurt if there wasn't anything there. After the mortician assured him that he had told the truth, Barker got back in his truck and left.

He anxiously watched the time and quickly answered his phone when it rang.

"Hello?"

"Do you know how many people in this sleepy little town are out in their yards this time of day?" Sarge asked. "I like to have *never* gotten away from the funeral home and then everybody I saw wanted to know why I wasn't on my bicycle!"

"Did you find anything?" Barker asked impatiently.

"Yeah, yeah!" Sarge answered. "It wasn't much, though. Just three of those sticks or whatever you call them. You know, those things that you plug into the side of a computer."

Barker asked "Have you had a chance to check them out?"

"Not yet." Sarge replied. "I'm about a half mile from home. Do you want me to have a look-see when I get there or wait on you?"

Barker gave the Ford a little extra gas. "I'll be there in a few minutes. We'll see what's on them then."

"Sounds good!" Sarge answered. "See you soon."

As Barker cruised down Highway 12 toward Hendersonville trying to keep his speed close to the speed limit, his mind was running wide open about Old Antioch, Lenard and Tommy Ray. It was a lot to take in all at one time.

"Ah, shit!" he muttered to himself as he recognized the Suburban he was meeting.

It was Tammy Reid and she had seen Barker. She flashed her headlights a couple of times and then shoved her left arm out the window and waved for him to stop.

Barker looked around and saw three or four other vehicles within sight and thought about ignoring her and driving on but the other drivers would wonder why he didn't stop. Besides, being on the side of a fairly busy highway should keep her from getting too bad out of line and he *did* need to talk to her but he *was* in a hurry to see what Sarge had gotten out of Lenard's hidey hole.

As Tammy's vehicle quickly slowed, Barker made the decision to pull over and see what she had in mind.

Barker pulled over on the right side of the highway on a wide gravel shoulder and Tammy pulled in behind him, her Suburban facing the opposite direction. She was out trotting to the driver's side of Barker's truck.

"Hey, Danny!" she squealed as she ran up and reached in the window, giving Barker a hug. "I was hoping I would run into you before long!"

Barker hugged her back, trying not to breath in too much of the ever present cloud of perfume. "It's good to see you, too, Tammy!" He replied as she held on.

Finally, after a long while, Tammy eased her grip, backed up a little and kissed Barker.

As he pulled away, Barker said, "What if your husband or his chief deputy drives by? This *is* a public road!"

"Oh, Danny!" she cooed as she ignored his caution. "It's so good to see you. I really need to talk to you about us!"

"Us?" Barker asked, genuinely surprised. "What about us?"

She reached for Barker's hand, which was resting on the top of the steering wheel and pulled it to her. "Well, it's just that you have been on my mind for a long time and now that you're back I thought that maybe we could, oh, say, work something out." He felt the warmth of her skin as she pulled his hand to the cleavage showing above the neck of her low cut blouse.

He smiled as he checked the highway. *Might as well see what she'll tell me about everything.* He thought.

"Something like what?" he asked.

She tilted her head to the left and smiled. "Well…I'm a pretty good looking lady who has a nice nest egg hid out and I'm stuck in a little Mississippi town that I *really* don't want to be in and you're a handsome retired gentleman with a home in Colorado. I was thinking that with your place out there and my money, why, we could be set up just fine!"

"W…what?" Barker wasn't expecting anything like this. "Damn, Tammy! This is , just, well…!"

She leaned into the window and lowered her voice. "Oh, Danny! You don't know how many times I've relived that day at the Christmas parade. Why, I even wrote you a letter telling you all the things that I could do for you…*to* you. I kept it close for years hoping to send it to you."

Barker soaked in the sight and smell of the very desirable female that was trying her best to get a real hand hold on him. There was no doubt; Tammy wore her years better than most. Her hair was shiny and bouncy, her body smooth and toned and her tits, well, they were *damned* impressive! Barker liked tits. Especially impressive ones!

But Barker was cautious. He hadn't outlived most of the other CGEs his age by being stupid.

164

He slid his index finger down the deep cleavage Tammy offered and watched her eyes close as she stood on her tip toes to offer more of her ample bosom to him, a sensual smile sliding across her face.

"What if I, uh, take you up on this offer and you and me run off together?" Barker asked slowly. "What's to keep your old man and that bastard, Pope, from coming after us?" He slid his finger across her braless boob and found her left nipple. "If you remember, that's part of what kept me from running off with you at that parade all those years ago."

Tammy arched her back, offering herself to the old soldier and whispered. "What was the other part?"

Barker smiled and answered. "I wanted to be sure you really wanted me."

Tammy's eyes flew open. "*Really wanted you?* Why, Danny! I've never wanted anybody the way I wanted you!" Then she leaned close. "*I still do!*" She kissed him hard.

What the hell! Barker thought to himself as he kissed her back. It was hot, wet and a hell of a lot of fun.

When their lips finally parted, Barker looked deep into the face of the former cheerleader. Damn! She *was* a good looking woman!

"So…" She started. "Did that mean anything?"

Barker smiled back. "I guess you and me need to start making plans. But what about Reid and Pope?"

Tammy grimaced. "Oh, we'll worry about them later."

Barker held his gaze. "Well, we don't need to wait *too* long. If I've got to kill either or both of them, I'll need time to sort of plan it out, you know."

Tammy's eyes cut quickly from side to side. "You, uh, can *do* that?"

Barker leaned closer. "What do you think I've been doing all these years?" Then he planted a quick kiss on her forehead.

"That's great!" She said as she lit up. "Can you make it look like an accident or something?"

"You bet!" Barker laid it on thick. He had indeed been trained in the fine art of removing unwanted growths from the face of the earth by the best instructors Uncle Sam had to offer. Hell, he even developed some pretty neat procedures that have since been passed on to operatives around the world.

Tammy Pulled Barker to her and shoved her tongue down his throat. When they finally came up for air, Barker looked up and down the highway.

"Look, we probably need to wait a while to get *too* hot and bothered." Barker said nervously. "We'll have all the time in the world to do all those things you've been dreaming about. But right now, we need to be careful, babe!"

Tammy shot a quick glance down the open highway. "You're right, Honey!" Then she gave him a quick peck on the lips. "I'll, uh, get in touch with you later and we'll figure everything out. OK?"

"Sounds good to me!" Barker said as Tammy backed off. "Just be careful."

Tammy paused a second, smiled, then turned and went back to her Suburban. Barker watched her wave as she drove away.

As he sat there and tried to figure out how to use this to his advantage, Barker's phone rang.

"Hello?"

"Barker?" It was Sarge. "Where the hell are you?"

Barker pulled the truck down into drive and pulled onto the highway. "I'm on my way. I'll be there in a few minutes."

Lenard Comes Through

 As Barker pulled into Sarge's driveway, he saw his old NCO standing in the doorway on the front porch.

 "Were you about to give me up?" Barker asked as he got out of the truck.

 Sarge had a serious look on his face. "I got tired of waitin' and plugged one of them sticks into my computer."

 Barker gave Sarge a long look as he walked up the steps. "Anything interesting?"

 Sarge gave his head a quick jerk. "That's one way to put it."

 A few minutes later Barker's attention was glued the computer monitor.

 "Damn!" he muttered as he watched the footage that was recorded in the embalming room of the funeral home.

 The screen was showing a well built, well dressed black man with his arms duct taped to his sides being first beaten with lead filled leather slapjacks before being laid in a wooden coffin. Then Ray Gantz leaned over and told him all about how they were going to close the lid, haul him to a little country cemetery and bury him.

Then he would lie in the dark and wait for death. While he was waiting, he could think about all the ways he had screwed "Mr Gantz" during the last few years of his life on this earth.

The man cried and tried to plead for mercy but Gantz wasn't interested in any of that.

Then, just before the lid was closed and screwed down tight, Gantz told the unlucky bastard, "When I get back to Memphis, I'm going to drive across the river to West Memphis and personally pick up your wife and those two daughters of yours. Your old lady'll be put to work in the old whorehouse over by the river. But those little girls, what are they now, fourteen or fifteen years old? I'll probably send them up to Saint Louis and put them on the auction block. Young, fresh meat like that ought to bring top dollar, don't you think?"

As he stood back and Lenard pushed the lid down with the help of two bodyguards, Gantz raised his voice. "You won't screw over anybody else, Tommy Tyler!"

Barker cut his eyes over to Sarge. "Tommy Tyler? That was Tommy Tyler?"

Sarge nodded. "Yep. Biggest underage flesh peddler from New Orleans to Chicago. Likes his girls to be school age, seventeen and

169

under. The feds have been trying to nail his ass for years. He sells girls to the highest bidder and they do whatever they want to with them. Some get shipped overseas. Most of them never see voting age. Tyler there came up missing a year or so ago. Him and his family disappeared without a trace. Now, you and me know why."

As Barker watched the coffin on the monitor being wheeled out of the room, Sarge leaned over and sniffed.

"You smell nice." He stated flatly.

Barker pinched his shirt just above the left pocket, pulled it to his nose and took a whiff. "I do, don't I?" he answered. "She offered to move to Colorado with me and pay her own way. All I have to do is kill her old man and her boyfriend."

"You did all this since the last time I saw you?"

Barker grinned and nodded.

Sarge shook his head. "You've been busy."

As the screen went dark, Barker told Sarge, "You better shut that down and we'll get them to Will. I'm sure he knows somebody that'll be happy to get them."

"Don't you want to watch the rest of them and see who else they buried alive?" Sarge asked.

"We can do that in the truck with my lap top." Barker answered. "Right now we need to give Will a call and see if he has anybody around that can take Lenard into custody before something happens to him."

Sarge was shutting everything down. "Yeah. You're probably right. I'd hate for something to happen to that old grave digger before he gets to face a jury." Then, as he turned and the two old warriors started toward the door, he asked Barker, "What *would* happen to Lenard if Reid and Pope found out about him?"

"He'd probably wind up in a nine foot grave in Old Antioch Cemetery..." Barker's voice trailed off and he looked at Sarge.

"We better keep him real safe." Sarge replied."His testimony will be worth more than a truck load of gold monkeys when the time comes."

Barker called Will as soon as they got on the road to pick up Lenard. After some explaining about what they got from the funeral home, Will told Sarge to send him the files and he would have somebody check it out on his end.

"Now, about Lenard." Will started. "Is he going to be a hostile witness?"

"I don't think so." Barker replied. "I believe all we'll have to do is threaten to drop him off on the town square where Reid and Pope can pick him up. This should be all the incentive he'll need to testify for us."

"What about the sheriff's wife?" Will asked. "Are you going to be able to get anything out of her?"

Sarge rolled his eyes as Barker answered. "He's thinking about putting something *in* her!" he muttered.

"I hope so. She's offered to let me take her away from all this, if you know what I mean."

There was a pause on the line. "I...see. Is that going to be a problem? I mean, is this getting personal, Barker? That can cause problems, you know."

"Naw! I'm keeping everything straight but I *am* planning to see if she'll give me any information we might use." Barker answered. "But right now I trust her as far as I can throw a Cadillac"

Sarge chuckled. "Give me a few minutes to get in touch with some people we have headed down there. If anybody's close, you and Sarge can load Lenard up and meet them somewhere on the road and they'll get him locked up. What about his family?"

"Yeah…" Barker drawled. "I'm sure if Lenard disappears his wife will be next in line for any retaliation. "

"I'll get started on locating her." Will said. "Any kids or anybody else we need to pick up?"

"His daughters are all grown and April is the only one that still lives in Mississippi, over in Tupelo." Barker said. "But she's the one who's digging the graves so she's in on this, too."

"I'll send somebody to pick her up after we get her daddy in custody." Will stated slowly as he tried to keep everything straight. "She might know enough to help us out some and she might be happy talk if we build a fire under ass."

"Barker smiled. "Maybe so.

Meeting Tom Tedford

Barker drove out Highway 12 and stopped at Tom Tedford's driveway. It was at least two hundred yards long with ancient cedar trees lining both sides. They touched above the drive from years of intentional pruning creating a canopy effect. They also made it a little dark and gloomy and it didn't look like there was much room to maneuver if somebody started shooting at you.

The drive also had enough curve to it to keep the other end hidden until you were well in gun range. Barker couldn't help but wonder what was waiting up ahead as he turned the Ford onto the gravel lane.

The old cedars needed trimming as they hung low in several places and the pasture beyond them needed to be clipped. Then the old house came into view.

It was a large, two story antebellum home with a porch across the entire length of the house and a small balcony in the middle of the second floor. It was painted white long ago and desperately needed another coat now. There was a huge chimney on either end built from brick that were made by hand from local clays. It had been a fine place in its day but was beginning to fall into desperate disrepair.

On the porch an old man was sitting in a rocking chair. He was seventy years old and his skin was dark from a life time of working in the sun. His blue denim overalls and tan work jacket were worn and faded.

He patiently watched Barker coming up the drive and when the Ford rolled to a stop, he reached over and effortlessly picked up a twelve gauge Winchester Model Twelve pump shotgun that was propped against the wall and laid it across his lap, making sure that the visitor saw this move.

Barker sat in the truck with both hands on top of the steering wheel and soaked up the scene. After a minute he opened the door and stepped out, moving slowly and keeping his hands in plain sight.

"Mr Tedford?" he asked.

"That's me. What can I do for you?" The old man drawled.

Barker nodded. "I'm Daniel Barker. I'm, uh, in town for my cousin's funeral."

Mr Tedford gave him a long, hard look. "Ya'll don't want to bury him out here, do you?"

175

Barker placed his hands on his hips. Tedford's quick wit impressed him. "No sir. We sure don't."

"Then what are you doing in my front yard?" His voice was stern and had no humor in it.

"Well" Barker started. "This is probably going to take a while."

"I've probably got time." Tedford's hands were laying on the scattergun just right to bring it up faster that Barker could dodge it.

"Mr Tedford, *part* of the reason I'm here is for Tommy Ray's funeral. The other part is about you…and your son."

The old man's left eye rose a little. "What about my boy?"

Barker chose his words carefully. "We're moving him out of Parchman, over to Atlanta to the Federal pen."

Tedford watched him closely. Finally he asked "Why?"

"Some of the people I work for felt like he was in danger over here so they fixed up some papers claiming Tommy stole some stuff over at Columbus Air Base and that got him transferred."

Tedford spit some tobacco juice off the edge of the porch without taking his eyes off of Barker. "And just who do you work for?"

"I'm a kind of federal agent. I do a lot of things. I'm what they call a Civilian Government Employee."

Tedford smiled a little. "You was in the army with old Mike Long, wasn't you?"

Barker dropped his head and smiled. "Yes sir. I sure was."

Tedford nodded his head. "Mike's a good boy. I hunted and trapped with his daddy. He was a fine man, too. Probably the best friend I ever had. Did, uh, Mike send you up here?"

Barker shook his head. "No sir. I rode out here with Sheriff Reid yesterday..."

Tedford tensed up. Barker held up his hands. "Hold on there, Mr Tedford! I'm not on his side!"

I sure as hell hope not!" Tedford snorted. "Siding with that sorry son of a bitch is a damn good way to get a belly full of buckshot! He set up my boy and sent him to the pen!"

"Sarge, uh, Mike Long tells me that there's a lot of crooked things going on around here. I spent a couple of hours riding around with Reid yesterday and I don't doubt it."

"Bah!" the old man scoffed. "That bastard's as crooked as they come. And he's had that damn right hand man of his, that Harry Pope, right next to him since day one." He waved to Barker. "Come on up and have a seat. I'll kill you later if I need to."

Barker climbed the steps and sat in a straight back chair with a split white oak bottom. Tedford didn't put the shotgun away but he did seem to relax a little.

"Tell me about Tommy." Tedford ordered. "What's this about?"

"Well, yesterday Reid said something about having somebody put pressure on him to get you to sell him your farm here. Sarge told me about Reid and just about everybody else being crooked as hell so I called a friend in Washington and had him check a few things out. I told him about Tommy and he checked on him, too. He felt like it would be a good idea to move him to Atlanta where his people can keep an eye on him and keep Reid's people away from him. They've probably moved him by now."

The old man leaned back and looked across his property in front of the house. When he spoke again, he sounded tired.

"That damn Reid's been trying to get this place for eight or ten years now. Says he wants to make a 'gentleman's club' out of it with all kinds of hunting and I don't know what all else. He says that wife of his'll fix up the house and have parties and weddings and such in it. Sounds to me like to me he's planning on turning it into a whore

house. Well, I guess his old lady could go to work in it right away."
Mr Tedford spit again.

"Hell, I'm the third generation of Tedfords to own this place. Tommy'll be the fourth." Tedford sat quietly for a moment, then said "Tommy didn't kill that girl. I just know he didn't."

"I want to get you out of here, Mr Tedford." Barker said.

"Nope. I ain't going nowhere." He raised the Winchester and sighted down the driveway. "I might miss a chance to shoot one of them bastards coming up that road."

"I'm afraid that something might happen to you since Tommy's been moved." Barker replied.

Tedford shook his head. "Nope. As soon as I leave, Reid will come in here and take my farm."

Barker leaned forward and spoke softly. "Look, it'll only be for a few days and Reid can't do anything that quick. Besides, if he wanted to come in here and do something to you, who's going to stop him? He *is* the law, you know."

Tedford rubbed his hand along the side of the Winchester and thought about it a while before saying "I guess you're right, but, by god, I hate to run away."

"You ain't running away. You're just moving over so we can do something with him." Barker tried to be as convincing as possible. "You can tell folks that you're going to Atlanta to see Tommy. I'll keep an eye on Reid and try to keep him busy somewhere else away from here. He won't do anything to the house. He wants it too bad."

Tedford thought about it for a minute. "I need to talk to Mike Long. I want to see what he says about all of this."

Barker stood up and shook the old man's hand. "That's a good idea. I'll send Sarge over in the morning. We've got a place over on I-55 you can stay at. There will be a team there that'll take damn good care of you and they'll let you know what's going on, when they can."

After leaving Tedford's, Barker drove around the county. He wanted to re-familiarize himself with the roads. He also wanted people to ask about the stranger in the gray Ford. After all, he was supposed to be looking for land to buy.

That night after supper, Barker got up with Sarge and told him the plan. Sarge thought about it for a minute, then said "Sounds good. I'll get out to Mr Tom's first thing in the morning and get him set up to move out for a while. I just hope this new kid of Will's don't get all flustered and screw anything up."

"Hell, he can't help it if he ain't had years of no holds barred combat under his belt like we did when we were his age." Barker stated. "He's got to start somewhere. We did."

Sarge thought about that for a minute and grinned. "Yeah, I guess you're right. "He probably ain't no closer to getting killed on his first job than we were."

Day 5

The next morning Barry showed up in town dressed in college boy clothes. This made Barker feel better but he still stood out since there weren't many college boys in Hendersonville.

They went to the Kettle to have breakfast and Barker ordered sausage, grits, biscuits and gravy from the waitress who had worked there for close to twenty years. She smiled at Barker while she waited patiently for Barry to make up his mind. Barry was looking at the menu as if it was written in Chinese.

"Is there a problem there, College Boy?" Barker asked.

Barry looked up over the top of the menu with its colorful pictures of different dishes.

"Everything has a lot of fat in it." He stated flatly. "And nearly everything's *fried.*"

Barker shook his head. "Not everything. There's coffee, water and, uh, diet Coke."

Barry was not impressed. "I'll just have toast." He told the waitress in a sarcastic tone.

"Would you like that with butter, jelly or dry?" she asked in a raspy voice.

Barry forced a smile. "Maybe a little jelly."

"We have grape, strawberry and blackberry."

Barry pondered this for a minute before replying in the same smart ass tone. "Surprise me...please?"

After the waitress rolled her eyes and walked away, Barker smiled. "You don't get out much, do you?"

The young CGE rubbed his eyes. "Why do you ask?"

"You look like you didn't sleep well."

Barry looked around the restaurant. "I got up real early this morning to check in with Mr Duncan's office and I didn't sleep much last night because 'Bubba and Irene' were trying out all the sexual positions they were watching on the Playboy channel in the next room"

"That will get better with time, but being rude to the people who are handling your food," Barker shook his head, "that's something you don't need to do."

Barry looked at him through red eyes. "Why not? I'm paying for it."

Barker leaned back and put his hands behind his head. "Because when you do, you might get a special surprise that the rest of us don't."

Barry's brow furrowed in confusion. "What kind of surprise?"

"Something like a big ole hocker."

The young CGE shuddered. "They wouldn't *really* spit in my food, would they?"

"Don't know, but it's a better idea to flirt with the waitress a little than to talk down to her." Barker answered. "You'll probably be alright. There's not much room to hide snot on a piece of dry toast, unless they put the jelly on it for you."

The conversation drug for a few minutes and the waitress returned with their breakfast.

"Here you go, Hon." She crooned to Barker as she slid the platter in front of him. "And here's yours." She said flatly as she dropped Barry's saucer onto the table with a *clank.*

The toast was smeared with a thick layer of purple jelly.

"Can I get ya'll anything else?' She asked cheerfully.

"No, I think we're just fine, sugar." Barker said with a big smile.

Barry said nothing. He just stared down at the toast, wondering what was mixed in with all that jelly.

After breakfast, they went by and Barker introduced Barry to the Sheriff as his assistant. The introduction went well and Ried seemed to be at ease with him. This worried Barker a little since Reid seemed to be taking everything a little too easy. Nothing seemed to worry him and a crooked cop, especially a department head such as a sheriff, should worry about everything.

"Do you have *any* other clothes?" Barker asked Barry as they left the Sheriff Department.

"Sure I do." Barry answered. "You don't think I came down here with only one change of clothes, do you?"

"That's not what I meant." Barker said slowly. "I mean, do you have any other *kinds* of clothes, instead of button down collars and pleated pants and loafers."

Barry looked a little apprehensive. "Aren't my clothes good enough?"

"Yeah, for Chicago or Ole Miss or somewhere but they're a little out of place for Hendersonville Mississippi."

Barry watched the locals on the sidewalks as they drove down the street that led to the business center of town.

"Oh!" He finally said. "I see what you mean. I need to dress like a redneck to blend in."

Barker didn't say anything for a few seconds, and then answered "Yeah, Barry. Dress like a redneck and everything will be fine. Just fine." Then he turned into Jenson's Men's Clothing and they re-wardrobed Barry.

Sarge drove out to the Tedford place early that morning. He hadn't been there for a long time and, even though the old farm was run down, it brought back a lot of pleasant memories.

Sarge's father and Tom Tedford were good friends and they spent a lot of time together, partly because they were both widowers and partly because of Bobwhite quail.

Rex Long raised fine pointer bird dogs, Tom Tedford had a wonderful quail population on his farm and both men loved to hunt. The two men, their sons and dogs spent many a fine day walking the fields together.

Tom Tedford was in his rocking chair as Sarge drove up the driveway and parked in front of the house. The old man wasn't sure who it was and had the Winchester laying across his lap.

Sarge saw the shotgun and called out as he ambled around the front of the truck. "You gonna shoot me or a mess of birds with that scattergun?"

A warm smile slid across Tedford's face and he rose to his feet. "It's good to see you, Mike."

Sarge looked up at the imposing figure for Mr Tedford was a few inches over six feet tall, a height that was exaggerated as he stood on the porch.

Sarge walked up the steps, expecting a handshake, but instead received a great bear hug.

"Have a seat there." Tedford said, motioning to the chair Barker had used the day before. "That friend of yours from the government was out here yesterday."

"Yes sir." Sarge started. "He told me you wanted to see me."

Tedford nodded. "Yeah, I do. Tell me about this Barker. Is he alright?"

Sarge nodded his head. "Me and him have been through a lot together. I've trusted him with my life a lot of times and I'm ready to do it again."

"That's all I need to hear, Mike. That's all I need to hear." Tedford's voice was strong.

Sarge sat silent for a minute before speaking. "Mr Tedford, I'm sorry I ain't been out here to see you. What's it been, four...five years?"

Tedford waved it away. "Aw... don't worry about it. We all get busy. Sometimes there's just not enough hours in the day to do everything we need to do."

Sarge hung his head. "No sir. You was my daddy's best friend and you was always awful good to me. I tried to come see you after the cancer took him but I just couldn't turn off that highway out there." He nodded toward the road. "I hope I can make it up somehow. Maybe by getting Tommy out..."

"You listen here, Mike Long." The old man's voice was stern. "You don't have to make up for anything. I know you miss Rex every day and I do too. And I'll appreciate the hell out of anything ya'll can do for Tommy. But you don't owe me nothing! Never have and never will. Now, you clear your head and do what ya'll gotta do to get rid of that crooked ass sheriff and his little gang." Tedford sat back in the rocker for a second before speaking in a softer tone. "But I wouldn't object if you came by once in a while."

Sarge nodded, looking at the floor. "I…uh…reckon I could do that." He slowly turned his head and looked at the old man. "I might even bring some good whiskey with me."

Mr Tedford smiled. It had been a tradition with him and Rex to sit on that very porch after a hunt and have a drink after the shotguns were put up, the dogs were fed and the birds were cleaned. "I'd like that, Mike. I really would."

Later Barker and Barry met up with Sarge at the pond outside of town and they talked over the plans for the next few days.

"This thing will probably go down fast if nothing bad goes wrong. Will's people are working on getting all the search warrants, arrest warrants and any other court orders we might need. When the G-men come in, it's going to be a coordinated operation. They're going to be in two and four man teams to arrest every county employee on their list at the same time so nobody has time to call anybody else and warn them." Barker explained. "They'll be the suit and tie guys so they won't spook everybody. The SWAT teams will be standing by just out of sight."

Sarge listened intently then asked "How are they going to make sure everybody is where they're supposed to be? Most of these folks come and go as they please."

Barry couldn't wait to get in on the conversation. "They all seem to stay in their offices until lunch so they'll be hit at 1145 hours."

Sarge gave the young Fed a sideways look. "Lunch?" he asked "Is that what we call dinner?"

"Well, uh, yes sir. I suppose it is." Barry said a little uncertain.

"Then why didn't you say 'dinner'?" the old soldier asked sternly.

"I, uh, don't know…" Barry stuttered. He was a little intimidated by Sarge, who knew it and fed off of it.

"Come on guys." Barker interrupted. "Stay focused! OK?"

Sarge grinned at Barry. "O.K. What about the Reids and Pope? I sure would like to have a hand in picking them up."

Barker had also thought about this. "You'll take a team and pick up Reid. He usually gets to The Kettle between 1130 and 1145. Barry will be on the team that picks up Tammy. They'll probably get her at their house before she leaves to meet Reid. Me and my team will get Pope, wherever we find him."

Sarge grinned and nodded his head. "Alright! I can't wait!"

The Flat Tire

Later that morning the weather was clear and cool. Kids were in school and most of their parents were at work so things were quiet in town. Reid was over at the courthouse and Pope was wherever Pope was.

Things were still moving slow but that was going to change soon enough. The teams were arriving at the farm and getting everything ready.

On the square the traffic was moving slowly in a small town way and Barker, Sarge and Barry were leaning against the bed of Barker's Ford having a conference. Barker was on the left side reading an article in the local paper about a farmer bringing in the first bale of cotton, Sarge was engrossed in a little yellow butterfly that had landed on his hand and the younger CGE was watching an elderly lady parallel parking in front of The Bee Hive, a beauty salon that seemed to cater to a clientele of advanced years. She should be through by supper time.

"We need to get somebody over to the Grover boys' scrap yard and see if they have any cars or farm equipment that'll tie them to this mess." Sarge said as he turned his hand slowly and watched the butterfly walk around on it. He looked more like a simple minded child than a trained killer that would be going to work at any time. "They're kin to Tammy Reid. First or second cousins, I believe."

"Yeah we do." Barker answered. His eyes were still scanning the lines of type on the newsprint. "What've you got in mind?"

"Let's send Junior." Sarge replied as he pointed a thumb at Barry without taking his eyes off of his little pet.

Barker cut his eyes over to Barry and stared for a few seconds. "Think you can handle it?"

Barry's eyes lit up and he snapped around to face Barker. "Yes Sir!" he answered enthusiastically. As soon as the words were out of his mouth he regretted sounding too anxious.

Barker held his stare for a long minute until Barry started to squirm a little.

"You're going to be on your own over there. We won't be able to help you if the sugar turns to shit." Barker said as he folded his newspaper. "The Grover's are two bad sons of bitches. Watch yourself."

Barry nodded eagerly. "What do I need to do?"

"Don't get kilt." Sarge said without emotion. The butterfly was still crawling around on his hand.

"That *would* be nice." Barker agreed." If you *do* get kilt, nobody will ever see you again. Those scrap dealers will see to that" Then Barker added. "Park away from the scrap yard and walk in quiet like. Take your binoculars and a zoom lens for your camera and try to shoot some pictures through the fence of any vehicles or farm equipment that looks too nice to be there." Then he got serious. "But most of all, be damn careful. Willy Grover is the big bald headed one. He can pick up a V8 engine and set it on a pickup tailgate and he can break a man in half in a heartbeat."

"And keep an eye out for Tuck." Sarge said as he watched his butterfly fly away. "He's mean as a cottonmouth and fast as a deer. But both of them together just love to cause misery. They was supposed to have beat Ty Smith to death down at Bo's Beer Joint but everybody that was there broke out in a bad case of amnesia when the cops came around asking questions."

"Don't get caught inside that damn fence! Stay outside!" Barker told him. "And make damn sure your pistol's loaded to the max and take plenty of extra magazines, just in case you have to fight your way home."

Barry soaked this up. "Is there anything else?"

Barker thought for a second. "Yeah, there is. Be on the lookout for a green 1979 Chevrolet station wagon."

"Seriously?" Barry asked.

"Seriously." Barker stated flatly.

"And as soon as you get through, high tail it back here." Barker added. "We wouldn't want you to miss out on any fun here."

An hour later Barry was driving down Highway 11 in front of Grover's Salvage Inc. The junk yard was twenty five acres fenced in by an eight foot tall cyclone fence that was backed by metal roofing of different colors and lengths standing on the ends. While it was kind of tacky and ugly, it was very effective at blocking the view of the eyesore that lay behind it.

A gravel county road turned left off of Highway 11 on the east side and ran to the back corner of the Grover property where it crossed another gravel road that ran across the rear of the scrap yard. A soybean field lay across the west side of the property so there wasn't much cover on any of the four sides.

Barry drove around until he found a log road that turned into a stand of pine timber where he could hide his truck. He pulled in and began getting ready for the recon mission ahead.

Barry had been told that the Glock magazines, which hold a maximum of fifteen rounds, should be carried with only thirteen rounds to cut down on the stress on the magazine springs. He pulled a gear bag out and topped off the magazine in the pistol and two extras. Then after a little thought he reached back into the bag and pulled out four more magazines and topped them off. "Barker's lived a long time doing it his way. Surely I can fight my way out of anything with a hundred and five rounds." He said to himself as he slid the pistol into his holster and tucked his magazines here and there. Then he slung his camera bag and binoculars over his shoulder and started toward the scrap yard in long steady steps.

As he walked along the gravel road across the back of the property, the scrap yard fence was on his right and a thick mix of young hardwoods was on his left. He watched this as he walked along and planned on stepping into it to hide if he heard a vehicle coming.

He also watched the fence for any openings which he could get a look through at what was inside but these were proving to be practically nonexistent. When he did find a hole there was a pile of something on the other side that blocked his view.

There was a pair of tall gates near the middle of the fence that were locked with a heavy log chain and a huge padlock but there was a small mountain of steel oil drums inside that he couldn't see around. After checking the rest of the back fence he returned to the gates. He was sure that he could squeeze through the opening between them but he remembered Barker's words about getting caught inside. "Just don't get caught." He said to himself as he knelt down and started to work his way in.

Once in he watched for any sign of the brothers or anybody else who might sound an alarm but it was quiet and no one seemed to be there.

The scrap yard was surprisingly organized. There were huge piles of different kinds of scrap metals here and there and heavy equipment scattered around.

On the west fence were a dozen or so nice cars and trucks parked in an orderly line. Barry headed toward them, using the piles of steel and machinery for cover.

The sun was high overhead and even though the weather was cool, Barry could feel the sweat running down his back as he made it to the vehicles and started taking pictures. Some of them still had the license plates on them and he photographed these and also the VINs, or vehicle identification numbers, which were located on small metal plates at the bottom left side of the windshields.

As he moved to take pictures of a very nice, late model Mustang, a larger vehicle nearby caught his attention. It was a green station wagon!

He cautiously moved around the Mustang and crept up on the large car as if it would run away at any minute.

Damn! He thought as he looked at the emblem on the grill. *It's a Chevrolet! How did Barker know it would be here?*

As he stood to shoot the VIN numbers he heard a deep country voice yell "Hey, you sum bitch! What the hell you doing over there?"

Barry's eyes shot to his left where he saw a huge, bald man with few teeth, wearing a pair of overalls and no shirt. This had to be Willy Grover.

Barry took off for the back fence gate but he saw a smaller man running faster that Barry had ever seen a two legged creature run before heading to cut him off. That would be Tuck. A quick calculation told the young CGE that he was not going to outrun this man, so Barry turned to his left and ran behind an ancient bulldozer that was parked near the northwest corner. He was hoping to find a gaping hole in the fence but instead he found a solid wall of steel.

He quickly took cover behind the bulldozer and drew his Glock. "I've got a gun!" he yelled. A second later the Caterpillar was peppered with a dozen bullets coming from two directions.

"We got guns too!" Tuck sang out. Both brothers broke out in laughter.

Barry snatched his cell phone out of his pocket and was met with a "No Service" message.

"Welcome to the south." He muttered out loud.

Barry looked around the left side of the dozer and saw Tuck moving behind a large semi truck. He was probably getting into a better position. Willy was out in front of the dozer and between the two they could put a bullet in Barry any time he stepped out from behind his cover.

And even though it was October, it was getting hot and humid. The sun was high overhead and there was no breeze making its way through that solid fence.

A few minutes later the Grovers opened up with some rapid fire shooting to let Barry know that they hadn't gone anywhere. Barry fired half a dozen rounds back with no effect at all.

"Well, I'll be damned!" Willy yelled. "He *does* have a gun!"

"Yeah!" Tuck yelled back. "But it sounds like a little 'un!"

This was followed by more laughter and another hail of high velocity bullets.

Barry's mouth was getting dry and he was now wishing that he had stuck a bottle of water in his camera bag. He also wished that he had stayed outside the fence like he was told.

He knew that Barker and Sarge wouldn't come looking for him until after dark. By then the Grovers would have him dead and stuffed into the trunk of a four feet by four feet by four feet cube of steel that used to be a Honda Accord. He needed to come up with a plan.

"What would Barker do?" He heard himself say out loud.

He tried to look around the left rear of the dozer and see where Tuck was positioned but this brought on a few rounds of fire from the smaller Grover.

Then Barry peeked across the floor of the Cat in front of the seat. He could see Tuck lying under the front of a Kenworth truck but he could only see his body from his shoulder blades to his belt and that wasn't enough for him to shoot at. If he missed, Tuck might move to a better place.

"Why don't you come on out?" Willy yelled. He sounded like he hadn't moved. "We might let you go…if we like you."

Tuck chimed in and Barry saw his body move when he yelled. "We might, but don't bet on it."

Barry decided to try something. "I'm with the U.S. Government. You wouldn't want any trouble with the feds now, would you?"

This drew another round of gunfire.

"Sorry!" Willy yelled. "We hate G-men. You can just kiss your ass goodbye."

As he sweated behind the Cat, Barry formed a plan. It wasn't much but it was all he had right now.

Let's see if this will work. Barry said to himself. He raised the Glock, took careful aim across the floor board of the dozer, and *squeezed* the trigger. The round hit the front tire of the Kenworth a couple of feet above Tuck.

It was quiet for a few seconds, then Willy yelled to Tuck. "What was that?"

Tuck looked around then yelled back. "Damn Willy. That stupid sum bitch shot the tire on this truck! He ain't much of a shot."

"Maybe his gun went off accidental like!" Willy yelled back. The brothers laughed at their own joke.

The tire hisses for a few minutes before Tuck yelled out again.

"Hey! Wait a minute!" There was panic in his voice. Barry had noticed that Tuck was lying under the front axle of the big semi with only a couple of inches to spare between his back and the front axle. As the air escaped from the bullet hole, it lowered the truck and the axle pushed onto Tuck's back, trapping him there.

"What's going on?" Willy yelled as Tuck scrambled to free himself.

"Willy! Willy!" Tuck's voice was full of terror now. "I...I...I can't get out!"

"Hold on, Tuck!" Willy yelled to him. "It'll be all right."

"Willy! Help! Help Me!" Tuck's voice was strained now. The air escaping from the tire hissed steadily as it lowered the weight of the big rig onto Tuck's body.

Now Willy had to make a decision. "I'm coming for you, little brother!" he called just before he started shooting, his bullets pinging off of Barry's cover.

Barry stayed down until the shooting stopped and he took a quick look around the left side of the dozer. There, less than twenty yards away, was Willy reloading his AR15 on the run as he tried to reach his stricken brother.

Barry took a quick glance at Tuck and saw that he was no threat. He was too busy trying to free himself. When he looked back, Willy was starting to raise the carbine. Barry fired two quick rounds, striking the big man in the chest with both rounds but he didn't go down! Barry put two more in him and he still stayed on his feet! He knew he was hitting the junk dealer solid but he got ready to double tap him again. Then, just as he pulled the trigger two more times, Willy started to fall like a big tree. He never tried to catch himself and didn't move after he hit the ground. This was Barry's first kill.

As he stood there, unable to move his eyes from the dead body in front of him, Barry heard a dull pop to his left. He turned his head and saw Tuck's still, lifeless body under the truck. There was a gurgle, and then a thick, red blob started to run out of his mouth. The tire was still hissing.

Barry suddenly felt weak and gathered his camera bag and binoculars before starting toward the back gate. He had only gone a few steps when he stopped and puked.

After taking a minute to clear his throat, Barry turned back toward the yard.. He didn't really want to, but he went back to the brothers and gathered their weapons. He then went to the front gate, pulled it closed and locked it with a chain and lock, similar to the ones on the back gate. Then, feeling that he was safe from any other intrusions, Barry went back and finished the job he came to do.

After he got everything done, Barry went out the back gate and walked to his truck. There he had a decent signal and called Barker.

"You've been gone for two hours. Is that good or bad?" Barker asked immediately.

"Good!" Barry answered, trying to sound cheerful. "I found some of the missing vehicles. One was a green Chevy station wagon!"

"Did you get plenty of pictures?" Barker asked.

Uh, yeah. I got plenty…" Barry's voice trailed off.

Barker waited a second before asking "Is there anything else?"

"Well," Barry started. "I…I had a little trouble."

"Are…you all right?" There was genuine concern in his voice.

"Yeah." Barry paused. "There were shots fired."

"Did anybody get hit?" Barker asked.

"Willy."

"Is he dead?"

"Yes sir."

"What about Tuck?"

Barry was watching a little yellow butterfly. "He…uh…had a flat tire."

Det Has Company

The next morning in Det's den, the old man was pulling his boots
on to go check the cows. The sky was clear but the air was chilly and
a light frost covered just about everything outside. He had gotten up
during the night and stoked the fire in the ancient fireplace and the
old house was warm. Tommy Ray's dog, Ranger, was stretched out
on the floor in front of the hearth enjoying the warmth.

It looked to be a good day but as Det was bent over pulling his pants
legs down over his boots, Ranger raised up and looked toward the
front door of the house.

"Something got your attention out there, old boy?" Det asked the
dog. He got up from his chair and walked to the mantel where he
took down the 1895 Winchester lever action rifle from its pegs
before heading to the front of the house.

This was a family tradition that Det's father passed on to him.
Friends and family came to go to the back door. Strangers and
dangers came to the front and you met them prepared for whatever
they brought.

When the patriarch of the Barker family went to meet his maker, Det took over the responsibility of protecting his mother and four younger siblings from the evil that might come knocking. It was never questioned why it was done, it was just done.

The 1895 Winchester Det held comfortably was a lever action, box magazine fed, thirty ought six rifle. He bought it in 1946 after returning home from fighting the Germans in Europe. He liked a lever action and fell in love with the cartridge while he was in the army. The only time it wasn't loaded with five rounds of the potent thirty caliber ammunition was when it was being cleaned.

As Det neared the door, he glanced through a bedroom on his right and saw someone moving slowly across the front yard. The old man stopped and, as the uninvited guest eased out of sight, Det quietly levered a live round into the chamber. He then slipped back to the den and retrieved his cell phone.

A second later Barker's phone rang. "Hello."He answered.

"Daniel. I've got trouble over here. I could probably use a little help." Det whispered.

Barker's stomach tightened up as he made a dash for his truck.

"Uncle Det? I can't hear you! I heard something about trouble! I'm on my way!"

About that time Det saw a second person climbing over the fence near the barn behind the house.

"Gotta go, son." Det whispered. "Get here as soon as you can." Then he hung up without waiting on a reply.

"Det? Det?" Barked called out. "Damn!" He pulled the 45 auto from under the seat and stuck it in his belt as the Ford screamed from having the accelerator slammed to the floor and held there.

"Now, you just stay in here while I go tend to a little business." Det said to Ranger as he eased the back door open. The guy coming across the fence had gone around the end of the house and was out of sight of the back door. This allowed the old man cover to get out of the house and take the fight to them, whoever they were.

Fifteen feet behind the house was a shed and Det stepped to the right side of it and waited, trying to watch both ends of the house for any activity. He didn't have to wait long.

Three minutes later, the intruder that came across the fence came sneaking around the corner of the house. He was a tall, skinny, white guy in dirty jeans and tee shirt. He wore a beat up black leather jacket and his scraggly hair needed to be washed.

His attention was on the back door and he was starting to place one foot on the bottom step when Det spoke.

"Hold it right there." Det ordered in a low voice, not wanting to alert this guy's partner if it could be helped.

The thug spun toward the old man, then froze when he saw the Winchester leveled at his mid section.

"Uh, ho… hold on there, old man!" He stammered. "You better be careful who you're pointin' that gun at!"

"No." Det drawled. "*You* better be careful who I'm pointin' this gun at." His voice was all business. The old man noticed the thug's hands were empty but there was an automatic pistol tucked in his belt.

The thug laughed nervously. "Heh, heh. Now I don't want any trouble here."

"Then what are you doin' here?" Det asked as his ears strained to pick up any sound made by the second thug.

This question seemed to make this one mad. "We ain't got time for this shit!" He spat out as his right hand grabbed the pistol.

Det held his fire until he saw the bad guy's fingers curl around the grip then, with the twitch of a finger, he fire the Winchester, sending a hundred and eighty grains of high velocity death into the thug's chest just below his sternum. The bullet tore through the organs of that area before taking a few inches of spine out his back as it exited his body. He was dead before he hit the ground.

The old man levered another round into the old rifle as he turned to his left and quickly stepped to the corner of the house. Being careful to check the area behind him, Det glanced around the corner before stepping forward and carefully and quickly advancing toward the next corner.

Here, Det stopped and listened. The first thug he saw was either around this corner or had gone the other way. He thought how nice it would be to be a young man again with a bunch of young, hard charging GIs backing him up, like he had done so many times on the way to Germany all those years ago. But now he was an old man all by himself.

Ah hell! He thought. *Nobody lives forever!*

Det took a deep breath before quickly stepping around the corner with his rifle pointed low enough that he could hit a man even if the other guy was bent low. As he made this move, the area just above his sights was suddenly filled with the body of the second thug.

As Det tightened his finger on the trigger, this boy dropped a pump shotgun and raised his hands.

"D…d…don't shoot me Mr Det!" he screamed.

The Winchester stayed on the thug as Det looked him over.

"Lonnie? Lonnie Wilson? What the hell are you doing here?" Det's anger exploded but his rifle stayed on target. He recognized the boy as a local kid whose folks lived only a few miles away.

"I uh… I uh…" He stuttered trying to get the words out and not wet his pants at the same time.

Det stepped closer and lowered his voice but not his rifle.

"Is there anybody else here?" he asked harshly. "Is there, goddamn it?"

Lonnie shook his head vigorously. "Ju… ju… ju… just me and Red!" he finally got out.

Det tilted his head to the left and squinted his hard grey eyes. "You better not be lyin' to me boy!" he said through clenched teeth. "If somebody else shows up I'll kill you first!"

"I, I promise, Mr Det! There ain't nobody else!"

Just then, the old man heard a truck speeding up the road, its engine screaming.

As he tightened his grip on the Winchester he asked Lonnie "Is that some more of your buddies? Am I going to get to kill your ass right here?"

As Det glanced down the hill, he saw his nephew's gray Ford come into view. "Sorry about that, asshole! That's *my* buddy! Now, turn around and start walking!" As Lonnie turned his back on Det, the old man reached out with a strong left hand and gathered a wad of his collar to hold onto. He pressed the rifle barrel into Lonnie's lower back and urged him forward.

Barker stood on the brakes hard as he approached Det's driveway, cut the wheels hard to the left, then hit the gas again just in time to power slide the truck up the hill, spraying gravel behind him. When he reached the wider area near the house, Barker stomped the emergency brake pedal and killed the engine as he bailed out the door with his 45 auto in his hand, ready to battle with whatever was waiting.

"Over here!" Det called out to him as he crossed the front yard a step behind his captive.

Barker scanned the area and ran to his uncle. "Are you alright?" he asked urgently.

"I'm fine, but there's one in the back yard that ain't! Here!" he pushed Lonnie toward Barker. "Take this slab of shit, will you'?"

Barker didn't ask any questions. There would plenty of time for that later. He took hold of the back of Lonnie's collar and they followed Det around the house as the old soldier led the way.

Det walked up to the dead thug and hooked his left thumb in his pocket while his right arm hung down holding his rifle. He stood there for what seemed like a long time, looking down at the dead, half open eyes that stared at something in the sky.

"This buddy of yours got a name?" He finally asked.

When Lonnie made no effort to answer, Barker gave him a shake. "He's talking to you."

"Oh, uh, uh, yes sir." He answered.

Det stood very still for several seconds, then turned his head to the left and asked "You want to tell me what it is?" His patience was running short.

"It..It..It's Red. Red White." Lonnie was obviously nervous and scared.

"Red White." Det repeated. "What a name. Old Dead Red. Is he from around here? I don't recognize him."

"Lonnie shook his head. "He…he's from below Grenada somewhere."

Det turned and stepped to the porch, took a chair and placed it a couple of feet from Red's body. "Sit!" he ordered.

Barker gave Lonnie a shove to get him started. The young thug staggered toward the chair and stopped at the back of it. Det returned to the porch, took a second chair and, walked toward the first chair. "I said sit!" he ordered louder.

Lonnie hugged the front of the chair, trying desperately to not get too close to the body on the ground before them.

Det sat on his right and laid the rifle across his lap, the muzzle pointing straight at Lonnie's belly, and announced "It's time to have a little talk."

Barker stepped to the edge of the porch and leaned against it.

Lonnie looked around at both Barkers and then down at Red. "Here?" he asked.

"Yep." Det answered. "Why not here?"

He pointed at Red's body. "Well, what about him?"

"Nothing like a fresh carcass to add a little atmosphere to a powwow." Barker said flatly.

Lonnie shot glances all around and squirmed in his seat. "Don't ya'll need to, uh, call the law or something?" He was sweating even thought the weather was cool.

Det leaned forward in his chair. "Boy! We ain't even gonna call your momma when we kill you. I've got a backhoe up yonder in the pasture that'll dig a hole eighteen feet deep. Nobody'll find a couple of bodies buried eighteen feet deep." Det's voice was strong and serious.

Lonnie's face began to twist and contort as his feeble brain computed this data. He looked like a little kid that had just been hit in the nuts with a baseball and was trying not to cry in front of the rest of the team.

They let him suffer for a minute, then Barker took a third chair and placed it behind Lonnie. He didn't want to be sitting opposite Det if that Winchester went off, either accidentally or on purpose. This kid wasn't big enough to stop a bullet.

He sat down, leaned forward and said, in a low voice, "I guess you ain't ready to die."

Through the snot bubbles and alligator tears, Lonnie shook his head and squeaked "No!"

"Then you better man the fuck up and start telling us everything you know about this little detail you and Red..."

"Dead Red!" Det Corrected.

"You and Dead Red" Barker corrected. "Put together."

Lonnie's shoulders sagged and he leaned forward, holding his face in his hands. He suddenly seemed exhausted.

"All I know is that day before yesterday Red came into The Six Pack and started talking about he needed me to help him make some easy money and he would cut me in for three hundred bucks. He said all I had to do was ride out here with him and watch the road while he shot the old man."

Barker turned his head to Det, who was intently studying Lonnie.

"Who hired ya'll?" Det asked.

Lonnie shook his head. "I...I don't know. He didn't tell me and I didn't ask him."

"You say ya'll was in The Bottoms?" Det asked. "Who else was there?"

The kid shrugged as he wiped his nose on the back of his hand. "Uh, there was a bunch of people in there."

"Anybody *special?* " Barker asked.

"What do you mean?"

"Anybody that usually wouldn't be there." Det chimed in.

Lonnie seemed to be thinking hard. "Well, not really. But I met Harry on the road between Tadpole Crossing and the crossroads but everybody else was regulars."

"Harry?" Barker asked.

Lonnie's head bobbed up and down. "Yeah."

"Harry *who?*" Now Barker's patience was running out.

"Pope. Harry Pope."

Barker shot his uncle a hard look and was met by his surprised eyes. "Why would Pope want to send this fucked up hit team after you?" He asked his uncle.

Det cut his eyes to Lonnie. "You got any ideas about that?"

As Lonnie slowly shook his head from side to side he began to shake and said in a scared little boy's voice that grew louder and more desperate. "He's gonna kill me! If ya'll don't, he will! Oh, lord! What have I done? What have I *done?*"

Barker's voice got louder and he spoke through clenched teeth. "Tell us what Pope has to do with this and we *might* be able to help you out a little, Lonnie. But you jerk us around and you'll be wishing Pope had you instead of us. You understand?"

Lonnie's didn't answer. He was sobbing uncontrollably at the realization of what he had gotten himself into.

"DO YOU HEAR ME?" His voice was loud and angry.

"I... I... I don't know if he had anything to do with it!" Lonnie managed between sobs. "Red just said I was supposed to watch the road while he went around back and shot Mr Det. Then we would get the dog and we'd get out of here."

"Ranger?" Det asked. "What the hell did old Dead Red want with that dog?"

The kid shrugged his shoulders. "I don't know. We didn't talk about it anymore. Red said he had a hot date with one of Bo's whores and he was looking forward to it. He was gonna get all coked up so he could really show her a good time."

The old man looked at Red. "He looks like a real Casanova!" He stated sarcastically. Then added, "I feel sorry for her."

"Me, too." Lonnie volunteered.

"Why's that?" Barker asked.

"Red likes to get rough with his women. 'Bout the only time Bo'll let him near any of them was when he wanted one of them straightened out."

"What do you mean 'straightened out?" asked Det.

"Well…" Lonnie drawled. "If one of the girls got out of line and Bo beat her up and the law found out, he might get in trouble. But Red never worried about the law so Bo would let him do it for him." He thought for a few second, and then added. "He was real good at it."

Barker sat still and quiet while Lonnie spoke, then asked. "Which girl was out of line this time?"

"Be careful!" Det warned looking hard at Barker.

"Which girl?" Barker asked again.

Lonnie sensed that their tones had turned serious and turned toward them. "I don't know. He didn't say."

Barker stood up. "Get up." He ordered Lonnie. "Uncle Det, I'm taking you and dog shit, here, *and* Ranger to the feds."

"What then?"The old man asked as he got to his feet and started up the steps to the back door. Ranger was still inside looking through the window beside the door.

"I don't really know." He answered truthfully. "I'm kind of making this up as I go along."

Det and Barker both had a lot to say to each other but they knew they couldn't speak freely in front of Lonnie. It would be best to wait until this young thug was locked up at the farm and they could get some privacy.

As soon as they arrived, Lonnie was thrown in a twelve foot by twelve foot steel cage in one of the equipment sheds. Then Barker and Det went in the house and let the Agent in Charge know what was going on. He dispatched a team to pick up Red's body and his pickup that was stashed in some woods a mile from Det's place.

"But why would Harry Pope want me dead?" Det asked Barker. "I ain't never liked that son of a bitch but we ain't never had no problems."

Barker nodded toward the hound that was lying on the floor. "There's your answer."

Det looked at the dog for a few seconds. "Ranger? You think this is all because Pope wants that dog?"

Barker nodded. "Yeah, I do. When I saw him in the hardware store he was buying chain. He said something about "picking up a new dog any day now"."

"Do you think that's what Tommy Ray and Pope got in that argument about a while back?" Det asked.

Barker shrugged. "Could be." Barker wanted to say more but didn't think this was the time.

Det leaned forward and put his face in his hands. "Oh, lord! He killed that boy over a damn dog!"

Det seemed to be dealing with a lot and Barker let him. After a few minutes Det sat up and looked at his nephew through hate filled eyes.

"You gonna kill him?" It was as much a statement or an order as a question.

Barker pursed his lips and slowly nodded his head.

"Planning on it." He answered.

"Good."

D-Day was coming fast and the Barkers, Sarge and Barry stayed there and went over the plans for it through the night.

The Tale of Barker

As soon as the banks opened two pair of two man teams came into town acting as bank examiners. They had a brief case full of warrants that allowed them to seize the contents of certain safety deposit boxes and other bank records from both banks in town. They took this material and drove like hell back to the farm on I-55 where a separate team quickly went over the Intel. They found a few items that carried enough weight to have arrest warrants issued and there were two judges on the premises who got busy signing the affidavits. Beechum's Livestock Auction Inc had been raided and their records seized. Pope had sold a lot of cattle and other livestock there and his name was on all the checks. It looked like Reid had set it up this way to keep his name out of it.

Everything was going well so far except the fact that the Grover boys weren't going to be much help. Dead men seldom were.

Everything was now coming to a head and White Oak County was going to go through a lot of changes real quick. There was no turning back now for anybody.

Sarge met with his team and everything was set to pick up the sheriff at The Kettle where he was every day before the lunch crowd and usually hung around until one o'clock.

Barry's team, or Team Green Horn, as Sarge dubbed them, would head out to the Reid hacienda. They would either catch Tammy there or on the road as she drove in to join her husband at The Kettle.

The Barker team's target, Harry Pope, wasn't nailed down to any certain place this time of day, so they were leaving early to hunt for the chief deputy. They would start at his residence and, if he wasn't there, they would split up and scour the county for him. Extra manpower would be called in if necessary.

Sarge and Barry were leaning against one of the Fed-mobiles watching Barker drive off with his team in search of Pope. Nobody was sure where the chief deputy was and Barker took it upon himself to hunt him down. It would be another hour or so before the others left with their teams.

"Sarge?" Barry asked slowly. "Is Mr Barker as tough as he tries to make everybody think he is?" Barry expected Sarge to come back with some kind of smart remark.

Sarge thought for a moment before answering. "Let me tell you a little story." He began. "Once upon a time in a war torn land far, far away a small army needed supplies desperately but the government red tape of this little country stated that someone of authority, such as a commander, had to request supplies in person to get them. So the commander of this little army walked through though jungle for two days with no sleep to get to a railroad track where he flagged down a train with the help of an RPG rocket launcher. Then he rode that train to the supply depot where he was able to get the needed supplies and load them onto a French made twin engine cargo plane."

"Now there wasn't no landing strip back where the army was, so they was gonna' parachute the supplies and the commander back into the area. But just before they got there an enemy rocket hit the port engine on that plane and it started a slow, banking, cork screw turn toward the ground." Sarge pointed his index finger down and rolled it in a circular motion for effect. Then he cocked his head to

223

one side and took on a thousand yard stare as he continued the heroic tale.

"That commander knew that if those supplies went down with that plane that everything would be lost, so he dropped the tailgate and shoved those pallets of supplies out and jumped out behind the last one."

" He was traveling kind of light and only had a rifle with a hundred rounds of ammo, a tomahawk that he carried everywhere, and a fifth of Irish whiskey that he had 'liberated' at the supply depot."

"On the way down he drank that bottle of whiskey so if it broke it wouldn't go to waste."

"Everything was going pretty good until he hit the ground and found out that he had landed right smack dab in the middle of two hundred crack enemy troops. Well, he shot a hundred of them with his rifle and he ran out of ammo. Then he snatched that hawk out of his belt and ran screaming through the jungle like a mad man attacking anything that moved.He hacked another seventy five to death and the handle broke. *Then* he beat and choked the last twenty five to death with his bare hands." Sarge fell silent for a few seconds and then looked hard at Barry.

"Now, do you know the moral of this story?" he asked.

Barry looked at Sarge all wide eyed and slowly shook his head.

Sarge held his hand up in a karate chop fashion and said seriously.

"Don't fuck with Daniel Barker when he's been drinking."

"What...? Wait! That was about Mr Barker?" the young Fed asked in total surprise.

Sarge threw his hands up in exasperation. "Who the hell did you think I was talking about?" he almost yelled. "Boy, you need to pay attention to people when they're trying to tell you something!" Then he turned and walked away, mumbling under his breath.

Pope

Pope's home was empty and there was no sign of his vehicle anywhere. Barker's team sped to a few other sites but the luck didn't get any better.

Barker split off from his team so they could cover more area. If one or the other found him, they would let the other know and converge on him together.

As Barker drove a stretch of empty highway his cell phone rang. He looked at the number and saw Reid's name.

I wonder what he wants? I hope he hasn't found out about today. Barker wondered as he answered it.

"Hello?"

"Barker?" The sheriff sounded scared. "Listen! Pope left out of here a while ago madder than hell. He says he's going to kill you as soon as he finds you. I...I think he means it!"

"How come?" Barker asked, playing along.

"I don't know!"Reid answered. "I just don't know! He's been pissed ever since you came back to town! He can get crazy sometimes! Mad dog crazy! I think he means it, Barker! If you see him you better be ready kill him! That's all that'll stop him!"

"You don't know where he is, do you?" Barker asked, trying to sound all macho. "I'll just take care of this shit right now! I don't like to have to look over my shoulder!"

"He said something about going by the gin to check out the equipment for the auction next weekend. Now, Barker! You be careful! If Harry comes out with a gun, you better shoot the hell out of him! He's a mean son of a bitch and he ain't gonna play fair!"

Neither am I! Thought Barker. "I'll be as careful as I can! Thanks, partner!"

As Reid hung up his phone and tucked it into his shirt pocket, a smile slid across his face. *This is going to be easier than I thought!* He said to himself as he took a sip of his sweet tea the waitress had just set on the table in front of him at The Kettle.

A few minutes before he called Pope and told him that Barker said he was an ignorant, inbred redneck and was going to cut him out of

227

everything. Pope blew his top and swore that he would blow Barker's head off right now if he just knew where he was.

Reid, being the dear old friend he was, told Pope that Barker was going to the gin to see what kind of equipment was there that he could buy with money he was going to take out of Pope's pocket. If everything went right, there would soon be two dead bodies out there among the tractors. This was just too damn easy! If he could have gotten Tammy out there, too, It would've been just about perfect! But he would take care of her later. Maybe a trip to the hog farm...

Reid knew Tammy had the hots for a lot of guys and he knew about her sleeping with Pope when she got on one of her horny streaks, but the local boys didn't threaten what he had with her. She loved the money and power he gave her more than she loved him. He knew that, but it kept her coming home.

But when Barker rode into town, he saw a big difference in her. She hugged him a little closer and ground herself against him a lot more than she did with anybody else. Then there was the letter. About fifteen years ago there was an article in the local newspaper about local boy Daniel Barker coming to town for a visit after retiring from service with the U.S. Government. He was only here a few days and that probably wasn't long enough for Tammy to get to talk to him but a couple of weeks later he found a letter to Barker in a shoe box in her closet.

It told him how she had admired his bravery and dedication and how she had always thought he was so special. It went on about the feelings she had for him and that she would do anything in the world for him if he would take her to Colorado with him. She could be ready to leave everything and everybody here at a moment's notice. He put it back and checked on it from time to time. It eventually went missing.

He also kept a close watch on Tammy for any sign of her leaving. Reid wasn't sure what he would do but he always thought it would be bad news for Barker if they wound up together.

The only thing in this world that Reid loved more than the money, power, and notoriety he was able to acquire through his job as sheriff was Tammy and he wasn't about to let Barker or anybody else take her away from him. He would much rather see her dead than permanently with somebody else.

Reid welcomed Barker with open arms so he could get close enough to get rid of him. And now, with Pope and Barker on a collision

229

course at the 430 Gin, he was killing two birds with one stone. Reid couldn't believe his good luck.

Barker wasn't far from the gin when he got the call and he headed that way. His team was several miles further out but would be there a few minutes behind him. He called them and told them to stay out of sight until he drove in and looked the situation over.

As Barker turned off the highway into the gin yard, he scanned the area for Pope's vehicle and any others. If this thing turned into a gun fight he didn't want any locals involved. They might be hit by a stray bullet or two or they might not understand what was going on and try to help their chief deputy by firing a few shots themselves.

When he saw the gray Yukon parked near the front of the gin Barker pulled out of sight between two John Deere combines. After a quick scan, he spotted Pope among the carefully line tractors and other farm equipment. He quickly got out of the Ford, his right hand pulling his M4 carbine behind him.

Pope saw Barker drive in and picked up the short barreled Remington shotgun he had propped nearby. *I'm really going to enjoy this!* Pope thought as he ducked low and watched for Barker.

Barker carefully picked his way through the equipment, getting a glimpse of Harry Pope every few seconds through the tangle of red and green steel. Pope was heading his way and was not being too careful. His anger and bully mentality was going to put him in a bad spot real soon.

"Barker!" Pope yelled. "Bring your ass on out here! I got something for you!"

"I'm right over here, Pope!" Barker yelled back. "Why don't you bring it to me?"

Pope's body was swaying around as he tried to spot Barker through the equipment between them.

"I ain't never liked you, Barker!" Pope said sarcastically. "You were one weird son of a bitch in school!"

"Weird?" Barker asked. "What are you talking about?" Barker wanted him to talk as long as possible and steer him to talk about Tommy Ray.

"I'm talking about that voodoo shit you did to my boat...and my car...and my *dog!*" Pope stressed dog.

Barker was a little confused. This conversation was heading in a totally unexpected direction. "Pope! What the hell are you talking about?"

"You know what I'm talking about!" Pope answered. "Remember when my boat damn near sank down yonder at Gum's Crossing that time? You was setting on your ass at the boat ramp when I got back. I know you had something to do with that but I never could find no holes or nothing!"

Barker laughed a boisterous laugh as he remembered the event.

"Aw, Pope! Didn't you ever listen to Ms Bailey in science class?" Barker yelled. "I snuck in your yard when ya'll weren't home and rubbed a bar of soap around those loose rivets on the bottom of that junky ass old boat. That soap broke the surface tension and let the water come in a hell of a lot faster than normal. That boat always leaked. They all did! But the soap made it worse. And when you run the hell out of it back to the landing, it washed all the evidence off."

Pope was really getting pissed. "What about my Trans Am?' I *know* you did something to it!"

"I dams sure did!" Barker yelled. "I dumped a couple of boxes of moth balls in your gas tank! They're made out of something that boosts the horses but it's rough on the rings. You burned that motor up!" It was quiet for a few seconds.

"Anything else?" Barker yelled.

"Yeah! My dog!" Pope yelled. His voice wasn't in the same place he was before. "What about Birdie?"

Damn! Barker said to himself. "You mean that sorry ass old shit eater you called a coon dog?"

"She was a damn good dog till you did something to her!" Pope was getting angry from the memory. "She was all tuned up and set to win that hunt!"

"Yeah, I did something to her!" Barker yelled back as he stifled the laughter. "I came by and fed that bitch a couple of hotdogs a day full of Benadryl for a week before that hunt. It dried her nose out so bad she couldn't have smelled a skunk if it sprayed her in the face! I can't believe your dumbass has been worrying about this all these years!"

"Now, you tell me something!" Barker yelled back.

"What's that?" Pope asked. His voice was closer.

"Why did you shoot Tommy Ray?"

There was a pause. "How did you know I shot him?" Pope's voice was uncertain.

"I didn't till now." Barker answered. "Why'd you do it?"

"He wouldn't sell me Ranger." Pope answered without hesitation. He was close now.

"You killed my cousin over a dog?" As Barker finished this sentence he started to move carefully to his right and took up a position behind two large rear tractor tires stacked on top of each other. They were solid and would stop anything Pope could shoot at him.

Popes voice was lower now. He was getting close and was trying to see Barker so he could give him a load of buckshot or two. "Ranger's a damn good dog and you know how I love to hunt." Barker saw movement through the steel of the machinery. Pope was getting close, coming from Barker's right..

"And I tried to buy him but Tommy Ray wouldn't sell." Pope was looking hard for Barker. "So I did what I had to do. Put the blue lights on him and when he stopped, I just walked up to the door and popped him in the head with my old Ruger pistol." Pope was bragging. "Old Lenard was there in a few minutes and we loaded

Tommy Ray into the hearse and pushed his truck off in the river. Easy as pie."

Barker thought about ordering Pope to surrender as he stepped into the clear but he decided against it as he took careful aim at his right shoulder and squeezed the trigger.

The bullet hit Pope deep in the joint, shattering the ball and socket before exiting the far side. Pope spun to his right as he dropped the shotgun and went to his knees.

"Stay down, Pope!" Barker ordered.

Pope turned to his left and looked toward Barker. He held his right shoulder with his left hand as the right arm hung useless at his side. His shotgun was only three feet away on the ground and his pistol was in its holster on his belt.

Barker repeated the order to stay down as Pope tried to scramble to his feet. *Oh well! I tried!* Thought Barker as he fired two quick shots through the chief deputy's right hip. Pope screamed and his body slammed the ground.

"I bet you'll stay down now!" Barker yelled.

Pope now tried to reach his handgun on his right side with his left hand.

"Leave it alone, Pope! "Barker yelled. "I'll be glad to shoot you again!"

"Fuck you!" Pope yelled as his fingers found the grip and began to pull it free. He then raised it to his head as he prepared to blow his own brains out.

"Can't let you do that!" Barker yelled without emotion, just before he fired a fourth round through Popes left wrist. This caused the joint to explode and he dropped the handgun.

Pope screamed like a wild animal, partly because of the pain and partly because of the anger of being caught with no way out.

As the now former chief deputy rolled around on the ground Barker calmly took out his cell phone, presses a button. "Come on in." He said to his team.

Barker walked to Pope and moved his weapons well out of reach then squatted beside the crippled deputy.

"Go ahead and kill me!" Pope yelled at Barker. "Jack said you were gonna' do it, so just go ahead! Kill Me!"

"Reid told you I was on my way out here?" Barker asked, halfway surprised. "And I was going to kill you?"

Pope gritted his teeth against the pain in his nearly useless limbs. "Yeah! Said you was crazy!"

"And I bet he told you to shoot me before I got you. Right?"

Pope gave Barker a surprised look. "Y…yeah. How did you know?"

Barker stood up as he heard the team coming in. "He called me and said the same thing about you." He stepped back and let the two team members carrying medic bags get to work on Pope while the other two stood guard.

He turned, walked back to his truck and headed to the farm. There would be a lot to do in the next two or three days.

At fifteen minutes before noon a fleet of black SUVs descended on Hendersonville and nearly every elected official was taken into custody, causing the rumor mills to go crazy.

Over at The Kettle Sheriff Reid had just ordered his meal and was sipping a glass of tea when he was suddenly surrounded by four heavily armed Feds. But what really surprised him was the fact that Sarge appeared to be the leader of this little group.

The old soldier handed Reid a warrant. "This is for you, Sheriff. You're under arrest." He said in a very serious tone. "Now please stand up and put your hands on the table."

Reid looked at Sarge for a moment and then looked around the small restaurant where everybody was looking at him, and smiled.

"Is this some kind of joke?" He asked. "If it is, it ain't too funny."

Sarge took a step forward and a second later Ried was standing on his forehead on the tile floor being handcuffed.

"Nope. No joke." Sarge answered flatly as he helped the sheriff to his feet.

Reid was then transported to the old courthouse and given a private room, with no windows, sparse decorations and a large mirror on one wall.

Over at the Reid home, Barry and three male agents and one female agent rushed up the driveway. Tammy was outside watering flowers with a garden hose holding a small, shaggy dog. When she saw them approaching, she threw the dog to the ground and ran into the house with the team close behind.

As she ran into the bedroom, she slammed the door behind her and scrambled for the bedside table and the stainless thirty eight pistol she kept there. As she started to turn, the door exploded as Barry burst through it. She was suddenly face to face with the young agent's .40 caliber service weapon.

As she crouched there motionless, her mind trying to decide what to do next Barry said the first thing that came to mind "Looks like you're between a Glock and a hard place, ma'am." She was cuffed and put in the big black SUV. The dog was left behind.

Barker didn't get in a big hurry driving to the farm. Pope wasn't in any danger of dying any time soon and Barker needed the doctors to patch him up and get out of the way so he could interrogate him. Strict orders had been given to the medical personnel to go real light on the pain meds at this time. They needed Pope's mind to be as clear as possible and a little pain could go a long way to getting the info you needed.

The medevac chopper that picked up Pope had outrun Barker to the farm and was sitting in a field next to the driveway when Barker arrived, its main rotor turning slowly. Pope was in the mobile trauma center being worked on.

Det was rocking patiently in a beat up old rocking chair that was left on the front porch of the house when the feds took it from the drug kingpin, his ever present walking stick lying across his lap.

"Come here, boy!" He ordered sternly as Barker stepped out of his truck.

Barker knew this wasn't going to be a pat on the back and a job well done speech. Without a word he walked to the bottom of the steps, stopped and waited.

Det looked hard at his one remaining nephew, took a deep breath and said through clenched teeth "I thought you were going to kill that slab of shit."

Barker took a deep breath and let it out slow. "I am."

The chair stopped rocking "How?" Det's voice rose. "You gonna *love* him to death?" Thick hate dripped from every word.

Barker slowly ascended the steps to the porch and leaned against a post. "Right now we need, *I* need, to wring all of the info I can get out of him. Then after he's not any use to us" he motioned back and forth between himself and Det, "He'll die. Reid will too,"

Det shook his head and rocked faster that before. "It'll take years for the law to hang those bastards…*if* they hang them! Hell! I'll probably be dead and won't get to see it!"

Barker stood still and quiet for a minute then said, "Come on, Uncle Det. Let's take a walk."

"I don't want to walk!" Det spat.

Barker was the one with the anger in his voice now. Through clenched teeth he spat, "Well, get your ass up and walk, anyway!" Then he turned and started across the yard...away from the house. Det caught up and the two strolled slowly toward the white plank pasture fence that bordered the yard a good seventy five yards from the house. There Barker rested his forearms on the top rail and propped his foot on the bottom one.

"Sorry about that, Uncle Det." He apologized in a low voice. "But there's too many ears back there." He nodded toward the house. "I told you that I'd kill Pope. Well, I might not pull the trigger but I'll see to it that he doesn't live much longer than we need him to. He's dealt with a lot of powerful people and when some of them find out that he rolled on them, *somebody* will take care of him...*and* Reid." Det was leaning against the looking across the overgrown pasture that badly needed bush hogging. He thought about what Barker had just said before he spoke in a calm voice. "This was probably the best pasture in the county twenty years ago. Old Dale Bratten owned this place and ran a big heard of registered Herefords on it. He kept it up real good. Pastures always clipped, barns kept painted, and these fruit trees" He pointed at the trees around them with his cane.

241

"They were always healthy and producing." He paused. "Now this whole place is so run down, it'll take ten years to get it back the way it used to be." He hung his cane on the fence, leaned forward and propped on the top rail just as Barker had.

"I know you'll do what you said you would. I guess I'm getting old and my patience is running out." Det dropped his head. "Can you forgive an old man?"

Barker reached across Det's back and squeezed his far shoulder. "You haven't done anything to ask forgiveness for, Uncle Det. Not a thing."

Then, after a few long minutes, Barker dropped his head and asked, "Uncle Det. Have you ever seen…*Death*?"

Det appeared to have completely missed the question and remained silent. Then, just as Barker started to ask again, he drew in a long breath and let it out slowly.

"I guess you're not talking about just dead bodies." He stated.

Barker shook his head and Det turned and looked him straight in the eye.

"Yeah. I've seen him." He watched his nephew. "You?"

Barker nodded. "He shows up from time to time. Usually when there's been a lot of killin'."

Det gazed across the pasture. "I was in a stinkin' fox hole in Italy the first time. There was dead from both sides all over the place that had been there three or four days." Det dropped his head and smiled a little. "That big son of a gun came right through there just a'swingin' that scythe back and forth just like I had seen my daddy cut oats before the war. He came right up to the hole next to mine and took that soul. I didn't even know the old boy was dead. Then Reaper looked over at me. Hell, I didn't know what to do, so I just waved at him. He waved back and went on with his work. After that I saw him around a lot of the battles."

Barker let this soak in a minute. "Did you ever *talk* to anybody about it?"

Det nodded. "Just one person. When we were fighting our way across France I got pinned down in a ditch by a pair of Kraut machine guns along with a an old nun."

" A nun?" Barker hadn't heard this war tale.

Det smiled. "Sister Angelique. She was a lot older than me and her English wasn't too good but with a little work we could figure most things out. Anyway, we finally got bored and I asked her about the reaper. She had seen him. Faucher, she called him. She said it was a *gift* that only a few people were blessed with." Det turned to Barker "What's your story?" Barker told his tale and the two old soldiers compared notes for a while.

It was getting near sundown when Will arrived and met with Barker. The Missouri farm boy had been keeping up with the day's proceedings and discussed everything with Barker. The day had gone pretty good so far and if Pope would tell them what he knew, it would be a slam dunk.

"Why don't I go on in and see if Pope's got anything to say yet?" Barker asked. "If he doesn't feel like talking now, he might after some of those shot up nerves start screaming."

"Sounds good." Will answered. "How about I drive your uncle out to his place. He seems to be getting kind of antsy sitting around here."

"That's a good idea." Barker agreed. "He'll try to teach you something if you'll listen to him, though. He loves to talk."

Will looked at the activity going on around them. "I could use some stimulating conversation. This place is running pretty smooth right now and I'd like a change of atmosphere for a while. We might get busy later."

Barker walked up the steps into the portable trauma center where Pope being held. It was, in fact, a pair of fifty four feet long eighteen wheeler trailers pulled in with a couple of big rigs and parked side by side. 'Slide outs', or extendable walls on opposing sides, allowed the trailers to be quickly linked together and become one very impressive, well equipped, high tech surgery suite. A third eighteen wheeler pulling a huge generator unit provided the power needed to operate this set up anywhere the trucks could go.

He was directed to a bed where a very tired and angry Harry Pope was lying, his leg splinted, the destroyed wrist hanging from and overhead bar and his shoulder bandaged heavily while the attached arm was strapped to his body to immobilize the joint.

As Barker approached Pope watched him closely. "Did you come in here to rub salt in these bullet holes?" he asked hoarsely.

Barker shook his head. "Nope. I'll wait till they fester up."

Pope winced as he tried to move. "These damn people won't give me no pain killers. I'm hurtin' bad!"

Barker crossed his arms as he stood beside the bed. "Tell me what we need to know and I'll get you something." Barker told him in an even tone.

Pope studied him closely. "Wait a damn minute! You're the sorry bastard that told them not to give me anything, ain't you?"

A smile slid across Barker's face. "I need your mind to stay clear. And besides, you might doze off if you get too comfortable."

Pope shook his head slowly, never taking his eyes off Barker. "Oh, no! I ain't telling you *nothing!* I know my rights! I'm the law!"

"Not any more, Pope!" Barker answered quickly. "And your girlfriend can't help you now. Reid and Tammy are both locked up. It's just you and me."

"You can just go to *hell!*" Pope spat.

"Whatever." Barker said as he turned to leave. "Just remember, nothing for the pain until *I* say so."

Barker drove back to Hendersonville and parked on the square. As he started up the courthouse steps, Sarge met him at the door.

"How did it go with Pope?" he asked.

"He's shot up bad but he's not talking…yet." Barker replied. "How's it going around here?"

"We've only got two interrogation rooms here." Sarge explained.
"We got a couple of good cameras and microphones installed before
we brought in Reid and his old lady. She's downstairs and he's
upstairs. There's two guards on both doors and guards around the
outside of the courthouse."

"There's a butt load of paper evidence in the conference room over
at city hall that came out of some safety deposit boxes at the banks.
A bunch of Will's folks are digging through that stuff now. Several
rolls of thirty five millimeter film have been sent to Jackson to be
developed at the crime lab ASAP.

"I'm going to need an office." Barker stated.

"Come on .The sheriff's office is upstairs." Sarge led the way.

Reid's office was one of the bigger upstairs rooms in the old
building. It was on a corner with four tall windows on two walls.
There was a desk facing the door and a couch against the wall to the
left of the door as you walked in. Book cases and a few chairs
finished out the furniture. The walls were accentuated by a few
pictures and awards hanging on the old pine paneling. A mounted
whitetail buck head kept watch over it all.

Barker walked to the brown high back, leather desk chair and took a seat. He leaned back, propped his feet on the corner of the old desk and crossed his ankles as he looked around the office. "It'll do." He said.

Sarge stepped in and propped his left shoulder against the door facing. "Do you think this thing is gonna' work out alright?"

Barker nodded. "Yeah, I do. It might not be just like we want it to, but it'll be alright."

Sarge's phone rang. "Hello?" he answered, then listed. Without saying anything he told Barker. "They want us to come over to city hall and look at what they've got."

Once there Barker and Sarge were shown piles of evidence by three of team members that were sifting through the paper work that covered the large conference table. Things were starting to come together. It wouldn't be long now.

After grabbing a quick bite to eat, Barker drove back to the farm to get any info he could from Pope. This time things were different.

Barker was surprised at Pope's appearance when he walked in. He looked tired and much older. A few hours of constant, intense pain could do that.

"Barker! You gotta' get me something for this pain!" He said his voice strained and hoarse." I...I just can't stand it!"

Barker pulled up a chair, took out a small recorder, a note pad and a pen. "All you've got to do is start talking."

"How much do I have to say to get a shot?" Pope asked, trying to bargain.

"Everything." Barker answered flatly. He wasn't making any deals.

Pope studied Barker for a few long seconds. "I can't tell you *everything.* I mean, there's just some things that I can't tell anybody."

Barker didn't move but he spoke in a quiet voice. "You start talking to me or I'm going to get up and go back to the courthouse. When I get there, I'm going to see what Reid and Tammy have to say. I won't be back before tomorrow unless I get everything I need from them. Then I won't come back at all." He leaned forward. "By then you'll be hurting *real* bad and they still won't give you anything until *I* say so. Do you understand me?"

"I ain't saying anything against Tammy." Pope muttered.

"Why not?" Barker asked. "She's not going to save your ass."

"Nope! No way!" he said stubbornly. "I, uh , love her."

Pope needed a little persuasion so Barker reached in his shirt pocket and pulled out the business card from Lenard's funeral home. He held it in front of Pope's face and watched as his eyes scanned across it twice.

"Recognize the handwriting?" Barker asked. Then he held it to Pope's nose. "Maybe you know that scent. She offered to go back to Colorado with me. Made it sound like a lot of fun."

Pope's mind raced as he tried to weigh his options as his body screamed out in pain. He finally seemed to come to a decision and asked Barker. "What do you want to know?"

"Like I said. Everything."

Time to Skin a Couple of Cats

The sun was going down as Barker got out of the truck and trotted up the courthouse stairs. The building was nearly deserted with the only occupants being a few armed guards and a small scattering of Will's people waiting on orders.

Upstairs in Reid's office Sarge was lounging on the couch when Barker came in and went straight to the desk.

"So, it went pretty good with Pope?" he asked.

Barker took the top folder from a stack of a half dozen on the corner of the desk.

"Better than I thought it would." He answered. "Is this everything we have on Ray Gantz?"

"They're still looking through all that stuff we've got at city hall and Will's got his people checking in Memphis but that little bit right there is some mighty fine reading." Sarge nodded. "You and Pope must've had a mighty interesting little talk."

"That's putting it kind of mild." Barker answered.

Neither man said anything for several minutes while Barker carefully scanned each page.

When he finished, Barker closed the folder and pushed it to the far edge of the desk and reached for another one.

Sarge swung his feet to the floor and leaned forward and pointed toward the other folders. "They all tie together nice and neat! Think you can get these two to incriminate themselves...or each other?"

Barker nodded. "One way or the other." He scanned a few pages. "You know that old saying about there being more than one way to skin a cat?"

"Everybody knows it." Sarge answered.

" But do you know the second part of it?"

Sarge thought. "Naw, I didn't know there was one."

"One of those old men that hung around Daddy's service station when I was a kid used it a lot. " Barker explained. "There's more than one way to skin a cat, but the cat don't like none of them." He looked over the top of the file at Sarge. "It is now time to skin a couple of cats."

After looking through all the folders and making several pages of notes, Barker gathered everything and stood up. The street lights were coming on around the square and it was going to be a long night.

Reid

The room measured twelve by twelve foot with grey walls and only a door, a small table and two simple chairs to look at. The two tube florescent light fixture above droned out a quiet, steady hum.

Reid sat in one of the chairs with his right elbow on the table and his chin resting in that hand. Everything seemed like a dream and he wondered if this was real or not.

The door opened without warning and he jerked his head toward it with a start.

"Hello Reid!" Barker called out cheerfully as he quickly stepped in and closed the door behind himself. He took a seat in the empty chair. "How's it going?"

Reid had an angry look on his face. "How the hell do you think it's going? I'm locked up in my own building by that retarded friend of yours and nobody'll tell me anything!"

Barker was looking at the folder he was opening and the notebook beside it. "Sorry about that." He said without looking up. "I'll try to explain it to you."

Reid leaned forward and cocked his head to one side. "Why don't you do that, you goddamn snake in the grass."

Barker looked up at the ex-sheriff with a grin. "Now, Reid! No need for name calling! Besides, it won't do any good."

Reid slowly leaned back. "Well, you do what you gotta' do. I ain't saying *nothing!*"

"Yeah. Well, that's what Pope said, too." Barker replied.

Reid's face took on a surprised look.

"Haven't you heard?" he continued. "After you called me *and* Pope and warned us about the other one being at the gin ready to kill the other one, we had a little shoot out and I won, of course, but Pope didn't die. He's shot up pretty bad, but holding back on his painkillers for a few hours convinced him to sing like a mocking bird on meth. So, you don't *have* to tell me a damn thing. But you're going to listen to *everything* I've got to say."

Reid crossed his arms and turned his gaze to the gray wall to his left.

"It looks like you and Pope have been busy since you were elected all those years ago." Barker started. "Doing all this hard work, cleaning up White Oak County and keeping everybody safe from all the thugs and murderers." Barker paused. "Oh Wait! That's you and Tammy and Pope and some of your buddies!"

"I ain't never killed nobody." Reid stated flatly as he continued to stare at the wall.

"Maybe not, but you've had Pope pull the trigger for you more than a few times." Barker didn't look up from the file. "There's a bunch of pumps out at your place right now draining your pond." Reid cut his eyes to Barker. "Now, what do you supposed they'll find when they get to the bottom?"

Small beads of sweat began to form on Reid's top lip as Barker went on.

"Then there's the election fraud." Jumping from murder to this caught Reid off guard. "We picked up all the elected folks that weren't legally elected here in White Oak County." Barker paused. "*And* the circuit clerk, you're Aunt Faye, since she set everything up. They'll make an example out of her."

"You leave Aunt Faye alone!" Reid yelled. "She's just an old woman doing her job!"

"And she's going to lose everything she's got and go to prison and get to take showers with other old women and be somebody's bitch." Barker calmly stated.

It was starting to get real for Reid. This morning he was the most powerful man in the entire county. He could take nearly anything he wanted. He could take a person's freedom away. He could even have their lives brought to an end. But now, only a few short hours later, he couldn't even help out the woman that raised him.

"You want a Coke or a candy bar or something?" Barker asked as friendly as could be.

Reid found it hard to think or move from the shock his brain had just received. He answered barely above a whisper. "Huh? Oh! Uh, no."

Barker went on. "Then there's the difference between your salary and what you spend. You have been milking this county like a Holstein cow for years. We've got IRS records that show, if nothing else, you're guilty of tax evasion."

"Then there's the boats and farm equipment, and guns and all that other shit at your place that belongs to other people. Some of it belongs to *dead* people. That don't look good for you at all!"

As Barker took a breath, Reid asked. "Why are you doing this to me? What have I ever done to you?"

"I'm doing this because you're a sorry slab of shit that's feeding off good, honest people that work like a bunch of dogs just so you can betray their trust in you as their sheriff and you and Pope and Tammy can have what you want. I'm doing this because I hate what you're doing and what you stand for and I'm going to make damn sure you pay for it with your life!"

Reid gritted his teeth and started to stand up. *"You ain't got nothing on me! Nothing!"* He screamed.

He was standing now with his fists planed on the table looking down at Barker, who was calmly looking back at him.

"Sit your ass down right now, Reid." He pointed over his right shoulder with his thumb. "There's two guys outside that door that would really enjoy coming here and watching you fall down over and over."

Reid's eyes shot to the door, and then back to Barker before he slowly lowered himself back to the chair.

As Reid leaned back and crossed his arms, Barker continued.

"Why don't we go back a little further? You know how you and Tammy used to let Pope drive ya'll around in your Aunt Faye's car and ya'll would get in the back seat and screw your brains out."

Reid shot Barker a very confused look.

"Then all of ya'll would ride around and drink beer and you'd get drunk and pass out pretty regular."

Slowly Reid began to lean forward.

"You didn't know that Tammy and Pope would drive up to the hay patch on Jim Hill's place and spread that blue Ole Miss blanket Faye kept in the trunk out on the ground and screw *their* brains out while you were sleeping one off, did you?"

Reid didn't answer.

"How do you think I know about all this?" Barker asked.

"Pope." Reid whispered.

"Like I said. A mocking bird on meth." Barker said as he gathered his files, turned and left the room.

Sarge came out of the small, dark room next door where he had been watching.

"I sure thought he would've been tougher than that." He told Barker. "Being able to hit him the image of Aunt Faye in the communal showers at Women's Prison got his attention." Barker explained. "And the details about the good old days with Pope and Tammy? Well, that's got him thinking that if Pope told me that, there ain't no telling what else he told me. His head's full of questions right now and there's nobody to ask."

"Mr Long." A young agent called to Sarge. "Mr Duncan needs you to call him ASAP."

Sarge stepped away to make his call and Barker stepped into his temporary office. His next plan of attack was on Tammy so he picked a couple of folders that pertained to her and made a few notes.

He would let Reid stew for a while and see that he was boxed in with no way out. During this time Barker would go ahead and hit Tammy with her first round.

Tammy

Will Duncan wanted Sarge to come to the Reid's for the final draining of the pond. It would be a while before he would get there and find out anything so Baker gathered everything he had and headed downstairs.

When he stepped into the nearly identical interrogation room her husband was in, Tammy jumped up and gave him a hug.

" Danny!" She squealed. "I knew you'd come! I just knew you would!"

As Barker steered her back to the table he said. "Yep! I'm here! Now sit down over there. We need to talk."

She scurried to the other side of the table in a child like manner and promptly sat down.

"So, what do we do now?" She asked cheerfully.

Barker took his seat. "Now, *I* ask some questions and *you* answer them."

261

"Oh!" Tammy cooed as she turned her head and waved her hand. "We don't have to do that!"

"We Don't?" Barker asked.

"No, Silly!" she said, playing the airhead role very well. "Because I don't know anything!"

"Sure you do!" Barker crooned back. "Pope told me a whole bunch of stuff you know!"

A worried look slid across her face but she tried to catch it. "Uh, Pope?" she asked as she placed her right palm to the middle of her chest. "Why... would he know anything about me? He works for my husband!"

Barker's voice turned hard. "Because he calls you the *real* boss." He gave Tammy a few seconds for this to sink in.

Her face twisted and wrinkled up a bit. "I...I don't know what you're talking about!"

Barker leaned forward. "Your husband tried to set me and Pope up so we would shoot each other but it didn't work. Pope's in a trauma center right now shot all to hell but he's going to live. I spoke with him a while ago and he told me all kinds of things about you and him and the plans to get Jack out of the way so you and him could have this whole county to yourselves. How he was going to be sheriff and ya'll was going to live in that big ole mansion out on the Tedford place." Barker paused for effect, then continued. "And he told me about your plans to fill in the pond and build a horse arena on top of it."

"Well?" She snapped. "What's wrong with that?"

"You're going to have to hold off on that." Barker told her. "At least until our people get through pumping the water out of it."

Tammy turned her head to one side."Pump the water out of it?" She asked. "Why on earth would you do such a thing?"

Barker nodded. "Yeah... See, they've been working on that most of the afternoon. Now, what do you suppose they'll find on the bottom of that hole?"

Tammy's bottom jaw worked up and down a few times as if she was trying to say something. Finally she dropped her head for a few seconds. When she quickly raised it back up she said. "I want a lawyer."

Barker gathered up his papers. "That's probably a good idea." He said as he turned toward the door. He wasn't going to call one but she could sit here and worry herself for a while.

263

Barker went back upstairs and got comfortable in the desk chair. For all of Reid's faults he sure picked out a fine chair for his office.

When Barker's phone rang he picked it up and saw that it was Sarge's number.

"Hello." He answered.

"Barker? Did Pope say when he dumped the last body in this pond?"

"Yeah." Barker answered. "About three months ago. The folks from the green station wagon. Two adults and two kids. Why?"

"Well…" Sarge drawled. "We've got a fresh one in here."

Barker leaned forward. "How fresh?"

"It's Lucy." Sarge answered flatly.

After a long pause, Sarge asked "Barker? Are you there?"

"Uh, yeah! I'm here." He answered.

"She's been roughed up *real* bad." Sarge said. "They're taking her to the farm to clean her up and get a better look at her. But there's this one thing." Sarge paused. "Your business card was in her mouth and her lips were sewed shut with electric fence wire."

"I left that card with Dolly at The Six Pack." Barker said. "I need to get over there and have a talk with her."

"I'll meet you on the highway and ride with you." Sarge said. "You'll need some backup this time."

It was almost midnight when the two old soldiers pulled into The Six pack. The parking lot was full of all kinds of vehicles and the juke box was booming from inside.

Barker parked the truck at the far side of the lot where the grass started. As they started toward the building the front door opened and an old drunk and an older drunk whore came staggering out holding onto each other.

"Come on Johnny!" Dolly slurred. "I've got us a love nest right around this corner here!"

As they made the left turn at the corner between the building and the pickup trucks, Barker stepped up in front of the happy couple. "We need to talk, Dolly.'

"Whoa there!" she said in a startled voice, then squinted her eyes and gave him another look. "Danny Barker? Is that you?"

Barker reached for her free arm. "Yeah, it's me. Come on. I've got to talk to you."

The old drunk whore tried to pull away. "You just wait a damn minute!" she said in a thick voice. "I've got me a paying customer here and we've got somewhere to be! *And* something to do!"

Her friend, Johnny, was only barely able to stand and offered no resistance as Sarge eased up behind them and helped him to a nearby pickup and lowered the tailgate, where he helped the old drunk take a seat. Johnny sat in the upright position for a couple of seconds, and then slowly fell to his left. His head contacted the steel bed with a soft thud and he was snoring almost immediately.

Barker pulled Dolly along. "This'll only take a minute. Then you can go through Johnny's pockets or…whatever."

In a quiet, dark spot Barker turned and asked Dolly. "Where's Lucy?"

She squinted one eye to help focus. "Lucy? This is about Lucy?" She looked at Sarge then back at Barker. "Hell! She's off for a few days. We always take off a few days and kinda' heal up after we get slapped around. Nobody wants a beat up whore!"

"Who slapped her around?" Barker asked quietly.

"What's going on?" she asked. "Is Lucy in some kinda' trouble?"

Barker didn't answer. "What happened after I saw you and gave you my card? You said you would give it to Lucy."

Dolly's eyes opened wider and she suddenly looked scared."Wait a minute, Danny! I...I just did what I was supposed to do!"

Barker stepped a half step closer. "And what was that?"

"Well, you see, Harry kinda' runs things for us down here..."

"Harry?" Barker asked quickly.

"Yeah! Harry Pope!" Dolly was talking faster. "And he came in just before dark after you was here. Well, I asked him if Lucy was coming in and he said she damn well better and he asked why. I pulled your card out and told him that you left it for her. Boy! He don't like you one little bit! He got pissed and *took* your card. Then he told me to bring her to Bo's trailer" she pointed at a single wide behind the beer joint," when she got here. "

Dolly looked back toward the bar. "Well, when she came in I told her to come on with me and we went back there. When we walked in, Harry was sitting there drinking a beer. He holds up your card and asked her what the hell that was. She ain't never seen it, so when she stepped closer to look at it he jumped up and slapped her hard enough to knock her ass down."

267

"What did you do?" Barker asked.

"Well, Hell! I got out of there and went back to the bar! I didn't want none of that!" Dolly answered. "I heard him hit her couple more times as I was leaving. Then she comes in a little while later and said she was gonna' be off for a day or two and headed out the door." Dolly looked toward the bar again and lowered her voice. "Is she alright?"

"Yeah. She's fine." Barker lied as he and Sarge headed toward his truck.

"Sweet dreams, Romeo!" Sarge said to Johnny as he passed the snoring customer.

Both men sat silent as they drove through the dark until the crossed Schooner River.

"Do you think Pope killed her later?" Sarge asked.

"Nope." Barker answered flatly.

"But you've got a pretty good idea who did."

Barker took a deep breath. "Lonnie told me and Det that the night before they came to Det's place Bo had Red straighten out one of the girls down here. Lonnie didn't know who it was but Red told him he was going to 'use her up', in his words. I believe Pope told his boss about Lucy having my card and the boss had Bo take care of it. Bo called Red and he took Lucy to the boss and they and did whatever else they did to her, and dumped her in Reid's pond. Then the next morning he and Lonnie came to Det's to kill him and take that damn black and tan coon hound back to Pope! Pope hired Red to kill Det and Tammy hired Red to kill Lucy. Tammy is the boss." Barker's patience was running low and his anger was running high.

"Damn!" Sarge swore. "Red was a busy son of a bitch till he ran up on your Uncle Det!"

"When I get back to the courthouse, I'm going to hit Reid with Ray Gantz." Barker said. "Then I'm going to pay Tammy another visit."

Barker walked into the interrogation room and found Reid slumped down in one chair with his feet in the other.

"It's hard to get comfortable in here." He said. "What time is it?"

"About one thirty." Barker replied.

"One thirty? When am I gonna' get out of here?" He sounded pissed.

"It won't be much longer." Barker promised. He pulled the chair out from under Reid's feet and sat in it. He took a picture of Ray Gantz out and laid it on the table. "Friend of yours?" Barker asked.

Reid glanced at it. "Never seen him in my life."

"I'm going to cut straight through the bullshit." Barker said sternly. "You worked for Ray Gantz in Memphis right after you and Tammy were married. Then you came back down here and ran for sheriff and won. I'm sure Gantz had something to do with that. You also own three empty lots in Memphis that butt up to three pieces of property that Gantz has three strip joints on. That's a lot of threes. And it makes you look like a partner of his."

"We ain't partners." Reid offered.

Barker laid a brass key on the table. "This is a key to safety deposit box 111 in the Southern Machinist Bank here in town. That box is registered to you and Tammy."

"Yeah? So what?" Reid asked.

Barker continued. "So, this box contains regular safety deposit box stuff such as a marriage license, deed to your house and a few other papers."

Barker laid a second, similar key on the table. *This* key is to box 374 in the Southern Machinist Bank. This box is only registered to you. In it are titles to cars, trucks, boats, and a whole bunch of other stuff that you shouldn't be able to afford. The IRS is very interested in this box's contents. They are going to look up your ass with a very strong telescope because of this box."

Barker laid a third key that was very similar to the other two except it was shiny and much newer. "This key is to box 1010. It's in the newer section of the vault at Southern Machinist Bank, hence its newer appearance. This box is registered to you and only you. Do you want to know what we found in it?"

"I know what you found." Reid's voice was hoarse and tired.

"Then why don't you tell me?" Barker asked.

Reid took a deep breath and exhaled slowly. "There is four hundred and eighty thousand dollars in it. There's no law against a man having some cash put back."

Barker smiled. "You're right about having some cash stored away, but the amount is off."

Reid looked up at Barker. "There was five thousand nine hundred and eighty eight dollars stacked all in a nice neat pile."

"Wait!" Reid was *all* confused. "I had nearly a half a million dollars in there! In hundred dollar bills!"

"Well, there's your problem!" Barker answered sarcastically. "The only hundred dollar bills were the ones on top! The rest were *one* dollar bills!"

Reid suddenly banged on the table with both fists. "What did you do with my money?"

Barker sat back and smiled as he watched the show. "*I* didn't do anything with your money, but I know who did."

"Who?" Reid yelled.

"Did you ever take that money out and play with it or anything? Or maybe you were afraid the cameras in the vault would see what you didn't want them to see. So you just came by once in a while and opened that box and stood there and looked at *all* that money. But you never picked it up to see if it had been swapped out for one dollar bills, did you?"

Reid's expression said Barker was right.

"This the way I see it." Barker continued. "Tammy knew that money was there and she knew there were forty eight stacks of hundred dollar bills with the paper wrappers with The Mississippi River Delta Bank logo on them. So she went to Memphis and got forty eight stacks of *one* dollar bills and twelve one *hundred* dollar bills. Then she came home and carefully slid a single one dollar bill from twelve stacks and slid a hundred dollar bill back in its place. That way, when she stacked it all up, four stacks long, three stacks wide and four stacks high, it took up the same space that your four hundred and eighty thousand dollars did. *Then,* she took your key and somehow got in there without signing the log and swapped out your pile of *hundred* dollar bills for her pile of *one* dollar bills. You came in, opened the box and looked at your stash, and only saw the top. Damn Boy! You should've checked the bottom."

"When the hell did she do this?" Reid yelled.

"Has Tammy gone out of town for any long visits lately?" Barker asked.

Reid thought for a second. "Uh, yeah. She went to her sister's in Miami last year about this time. Sis was real sick and Tammy helped out down there for, uh, about three weeks...or so."

Barker looked back at the file. "That explains it."

"Explains what?" Reid asked, trying to see what Barker was looking at.

Barker took another key and laid it next the other three. It was similar but clearly didn't belong with the others.

"This is key to box 286 from The Mississippi Agriculture and Forestry Bank, also here in town." Barker stated in a calm even voice. "This box isn't in your name. It's in your wife's name." He leaned forward. "In this box we found a whole bunch of neat stuff, including your money less about eighty thousand dollars. But we did find a deed in there for a condo that was bought in Cancun Mexico on September thirty first of last year. The owners were one Tammy Reid…" Barker paused just to torture Reid. "And one Silvie Tower." Reid's jaw tightened up and his face began to turn red.

"And here's a picture of the happy couple!" Barker pulled out a picture of Tammy and Sylvie lying together in each other's arms in almost nothing bikinis on a chaise lounge on a white sand beach with beautiful blue water in the background.

Barker was sure Reid was going to come unglued but he suddenly looked very tired, propped his elbows on the table and rested his head in his hands.

"Now, this, along with the fact that you not only investigated this girl's murder, but also testified against the Tedford kid for killing your wife's girlfriend is mighty suspicious."

"I can't believe she stole *my* money." Reid muttered.

"That's not your money. Not anymore." Barker said.

Reid looked up. "The hell it ain't!"

"Nope. It's all been seized." Barker told him. "All of your assets and those of anybody you might be in any partnership with, have been frozen until all cases against you have been settled." Barker announced.

"You can't do that!" Reid's voice rose. "I need that money to…to pay bills and to, uh…"

"Pay lawyers!" Barker helped.

"Well, yeah!"Reid sounded worried.

Barker shook his head. "It ain't going to happen, Reid. As I said, *all* of your assets *and* those of your partners have been frozen until…" He shrugged his shoulders.

Reid thought quickly. "What…what partners?"

Barker leaned back, put his arms above his head and stretched his cramped muscles. "There's Tammy. And there's Pope. You know, all of ya'll are being charged with some of the same crimes and that makes partners of some kind." He lowered his arms and crossed them across his chest. "But most of all, there's Ray Gantz."

Reid froze and seemed to stop breathing. "Ray Gantz? But...but we're not partners."

"It really doesn't matter." Barker's voice was very, very cold. "With you owning those properties next to his, we won't have any trouble convincing the judges that you bought that land so Gantz could expand his titty bars and you would profit from that, making you and him" Barker held up two fingers on each hand to simulate quotation marks, "'partners'." Barker leaned forward. "Are you familiar with the term 'tainted money'?"

Reid shook his head slowly.

"With you and him being partners, your money could've mingled with his somewhere along the way. If this happened, it would be impossible to discern between Gantz's money and yours. And since *your* assets, *all* your assets, are being frozen, Gantz assets, *all* of his assets, will also be frozen until he can prove that his assets aren't tainted by your dirty ass money. That means that his titty bars and any other businesses that he has money borrowed on, will be locked up ASAP as part of his assets. And that could take years. A lot of years." Barker paused. "Do you think Mr Gantz will be happy with that?"

Reid shook his head rapidly and he began to stutter. "N… no! Y…y…you can't do this! He'll…he'll…he'll kill me!"

Barker's expression didn't change. "Maybe he'll bury you out at Old Antioch."

Reid's eyes locked onto Barker's and the color drained from his face.

"I told you Pope sang loud and clear." Barker said flatly. "When I asked him how he got Lenard to take Tommy Ray in at the funeral home with a bullet in his head and not say anything, he told me all about Gantz bringing a body down here once in a while when he needed to get rid of it. And he told me all about Lenard putting them in a casket and ya'll burying them out at Old Antioch."

And then with Lenard giving us the videos of ya'll putting those people in the coffins, well that was just icing on the cake."

"That was a damn good idea. Nobody's been buried out there in years and nobody would come looking for them. And he told me that Lenard would take care of the dearly unwanted if he was still breathing when he got here, for a fee, of course." Barker gave this a second to sink in. "Now, do you think Lenard is going to take the heat for you, or squeal like a pig if he's offered a deal to save his own ass?"

Reid was starting to shake and sweat. Things just went from bad to a whole lot worse.

Barker closed the folder and stood up.

"I'm going to give you a little while to think about what you need to do." Barker said as he looked down at Reid. "We're going to turn you lose later today. You won't have any money or a house or a truck or any friends. You *will* have a very angry Ray Gantz after your ass. Think about it."

Barker turned and left the room.

It was two thirty five when Barker walked into the office and sat down in the comfortable chair again. His feet automatically went to the desk top.

It had been a long day and it wasn't over yet but it was getting closer all the time.

He closed his eyes and prepared to rest his them for a few minutes when he heard boots coming down the hall.

"Barker?" Sarge asked. "You awake?"

Barker took a deep breath and let it out slow but he didn't open his eyes. "Yeah. What ya' got?"

Sarge dropped a folder on the desk and laid a cell phone beside it. Then he turned and fell back on the couch and pulled his cap down over his eyes.

Barker slowly lowered his feet to the floor and reached for the folder. He held it up in front of himself and stared at Lucy Waits' name on the tab before dropping it on the desk and opening it up. After scanning the pages inside, he lowered his head and said a silent prayer.

"I never said it was *good* news." Sarge commented. "You sure had it figured right." Then, after a pause he added "I'm sorry, Cap'n."

Barker got wearily to his feet. As he started out the door he muttered. "It's time to finish this shit."

Tammy was asleep at the table on her crossed arms when Barker stormed into the small, grey room and slammed the folder onto the table in front of her, causing her to sit up with a jerk. He quickly sat in the chair across the table.

The long day was taking its toll on her, her makeup smeared and her hair frizzed.

"Tell me about Lucy Waits." He ordered.

"Who?" She asked innocently.

"Lucy Waits!" Barker repeated louder.

Tammy rubbed the side of her face with the palm of her right hand. "Lucy? I don't think I know any…"

Barker slammed a photo of Lucy's dead face on the table in front of her. There were nine loops of wire passing through her lips. They were each neatly twisted together in front. Her face was bruised and swollen from a terrible beating but the notes from the coroner stated that she was still alive when she was dumped in the pond with the concrete block tied to her neck . This meant she was also alive when her mouth was sewed shut.

"It's been a long day, I'm tired and you just need to sit on your ass and listen!" Barker was angry and it scared Tammy.

"I went to The Six Pack and left a card for Lucy. Pope found out and slapped her around some. *Then* he told you about it. You called Bo Roberts and told him to get Lucy over to your place so he had Red White pick her up."

Tammy looked surprised. *How could he know about that?* She wondered.

"Red brought her to your horse barn where ya'll raped her and tortured her. But before you rolled her off your pontoon boat into your pond, you shoved my card in her mouth and sewed her lips together with electric fence wire."

"That's a wild story you've got there!" Tammy suddenly shouted. "And you can't prove that I had a damn thing to do with Lucy! Not a damn thing!"

Barker reached into his shirt pocket and snatched out the cell phone Sarge dropped off, pushed a button and held it up so Tammy could watch the video recorded on it.

It showed Tammy beating Lucy's naked body with a four feet long piece of steel concrete reinforcement rod while her hands were tied over her head, Barker said, "Smile! You're on candid camera, bitch! And Red shot a bunch of video of you doing what you did! He even shot some of you pushing her off the deck of your pontoon boat with that block tied to her neck...the same block she was found tied to a little while ago! You are screwed!"

He pocketed the phone, grabbed his folder, got up and turned to the door..

"She didn't have any right to you!" Tammy yelled as she jumped to her feet.

Barker stopped and slowly turned around. In a tone full of hate, asked simply, "What?"

"I wanted you! The only reason I ever married Jack was he had everything set up to go to work for Ray up in Memphis! We were going to make big money and party with popular people and live in a big, fancy house!" Her anger grew as she went. "But then they hatched that plan for us to move back down here and for Jack to run for sheriff so they could run the damn county! So we've been here in the sticks with the hicks ever since! You were the only person who ever got out of here and stayed out! I wanted to get out of here with you but it never came to be!"

Barker stepped closer and his best sympathetic voice, said. "Why, Tammy! I...I never knew!"

"Oh, Danny!" She cooed! "So you can get me out of here?"

Barker looked deep into her eyes, took a deep breath as he leaned closer and said..."Go to hell, bitch!" It only took two steps and he was in the hall headed for the stairs. Her screaming and cussing faded behind him.

Barker found Reid rocking back and forth on the back legs of his chair. He seemed to be sliding into a deep depression.

"He'll kill me, Barker." Reid said before the door was closed. He rubbed his forehead with a shaking hand. "Gantz is going to kill me. Even if I go to prison, he'll get somebody to kill me on the inside."

Barker didn't bother to sit down and the cameras and recorders weren't on.

"You're right. You are absolutely right." Barker stared at the totally broken man before him. A single day sure made a lot of difference. "You know that old thirty eight in your desk drawer?"

Reid thought a second. "Yeah. It was my Dad's. I... I keep it in there for luck."

Barker leaned close and spoke in a low tone. "Well, your luck just ran out. It has one bullet in it. I'm sure if you asked real nice the guards will let you go to your office for a few minutes to clean up or something." He leaned closer. "Don't fuck it up."

Reid thought for a few seconds, then looked up at Barker, nodded and looked back down at the table.

Barker turned and left the room for the last time.

He went downstairs and stepped out in the fresh, cool air. The sky was lit up in the east with streaks of pink and orange announcing the beginning of another day in the sunny south.

"Hey, Barker!" Sarge called from the corner of the square. Will Duncan and Barry Watson were with him.

Barker walked to them and they talked about the long night that now seemed to be behind them.

"It looks like we've got everything we need to convict all the three of them." Will said as he nodded toward the courthouse. "I'm sure the DA's will work something out with everybody else. I was afraid Tammy might be able to make a deal until we found out about Lucy Waits. By the way, I'm sorry about her."

"Me too." Barker answered. "I don't know what Tommy Ray had to do with her, but this whole mess would still be running wide open if he had sold that coon dog to Pope."

They all agreed and started toward The Kettle to get an early breakfast when a muffled shot came from the courthouse.

A minute later an agent ran out of the door and looked around the square. When he saw Will, he ran over.

"Mr Duncan!" he said as he came close. "Sheriff Reid just shot himself in his office!"

Will glanced at Barker. "Is he OK?"

The agent shook his head. "No sir."

The agent turned to go back inside, then stopped and turned back to them.

"Mr Barker! I almost forgot!" He said. "The doctor that's taking care of Deputy Pope called. It seems that a blood clot probably broke free and caused a problem with a heart valve. He died about a half hour ago."

An hour later, Sarge, Barker, Will and Barry had finished their breakfast and were leaving the restaurant to get some rest. As Barker paid at the cash register, an old friend came in.

"Danny Barker?" She asked. "How long have you been in town?"

A lot had happened in the short time since he arrived. "A few days." He answered. "Just a few days."

I

David Box is a native of Bruce, Mississippi. He later moved to Oxford, Mississippi and lived there for several years. He and his wife Yvonne have four children, Rachelle, Jarod, Laura and Joseph and three grandchildren, Makyah, Tobias and Dorien.

He was a Deputy Sheriff for 18 years in Lafayette County, Mississippi. When he retired, he moved to Evanston, Wyoming with Yvonne, where he loves living out west.

David has had several articles published in BackWoodsMan Magazine over the years. He loves writing about what he knows.

You can reach him by e-mail at boxrange@aol.com.

Made in the USA
Charleston, SC
12 January 2017